I0592682

Her Outback Playboy

Annie Seaton

Second Chance Bay Series

Her Outback Playboy

Her Outback Protector

Her Outback Haven

Her Outback Paradise

Dedication

This book is dedicated to the wonderful readers we meet on the road as I research my books!

Chapter One

Jake Jones stood on the bridge of his sleek white motor cruiser as it approached the mouth of the Norman River. He closed his eyes and lifted his face to the salt-laden air and took a deep breath. The fresh clean smell of the coast and the sharp tang of the mangroves soothed him. Ten years away from home had been way too long.

The smell of this landscape; there was nothing like it.

No matter where Jake had been in his time away, he'd never smelled sweet, untouched salt air like that of the Gulf of Carpentaria. He stood, unmoving, absorbing the familiar sounds and smells for a few minutes before he opened his eyes again. Ahead the short stubby mangroves covered the edge of the water like a dark green curtain as the sun sank low in the winter sky. The waters of the Gulf glinted silver as the light faded in the gathering dusk. There was no movement apart from the water birds pecking around the tree roots sending sea creatures scurrying for shelter. In the distance shards of sunlight glinted off the rod of a lone fisherman on the point. This was not a pretty coastline like the surf beaches of the east coast of Australia, nor did it have the rugged grandeur of the Mediterranean, but it was quiet and serene.

And it was home.

Monaco had been pretty, and the boats at Monte Carlo had been luxurious, but the smell of diesel and petrol had always hung in the air around the huge marina. It had been noisy and busy no matter what the hour and the hum of traffic around the harbour was constant. Last winter it had been the smell of snow covering Mont Agel above the harbour that had filled Jake with homesickness until he'd decided it was time to go home.

Almost. He wasn't going to return to the town that he had left beneath a cloud of shame until he could return triumphant. He'd had to put some final business plans in place, and when everything was settled, he made his move to come home. He was coming back to Second Chance Bay on his terms; it had taken a long time to get himself to the position when he was confident enough to come back to the Bay. He had a lot to prove to the community he'd left behind as a young man almost ten years ago.

'Do you want me to berth at the docks over town?' Gus, his deckhand, gestured with his head to the dock ahead. They'd picked up *Moonshine*, one of his new motor cruisers in Darwin, and it had taken a couple of days for the paperwork to be organised before they'd headed east along the coast to Second Chance Bay. Jake had booked a helicopter to fly Gus back to Darwin tomorrow to pick up the second charter boat he'd bought. Gus would be bringing the rest of the crew with him on the way back. The first charter was already booked and filled with the maximum number of clients on each vessel.

Jake had ticked all the boxes and had organised every last facet of his business before he'd come home. He wasn't leaving himself open to any criticism.

He was successful, and he wanted the town to see that.

With a shake of his head, he answered Gus. 'No. Keep going. We'll refuel in town tomorrow. I'm keen to get berthed. I have a visit to make.'

'Rightio, captain.' Gus saluted with a wide grin.

'Piss off, Gus. You can cut the captain stuff.' He knew Gus was teasing him, but he wasn't in the mood. Even though he was trying hard to look calm on the outside, coming home to the town that had done him so much damage made his gut churn.

Jake stared at the hotel on the point at Karumba as they approached the entrance to the river. Second Chance Bay was a small village across the river from Karumba, a town famous for its sunsets and not much else, apart from the prawn industry.

Unless you counted its fame for being the place where Jake had lost his dreams along with the respect of the people who were important to him, but that was something he didn't talk about. But when the time to travel back approached, the memories of the past had filled his waking hours and his dreams.

'You really grew up here?' Gus looked at him and his face was a study in disbelief.

Jake nodded. 'Sure did. What's the problem with that?'

Gus shrugged. 'Doesn't seem to be much around here. Always had the impression you were a city boy. You know, learned to sail in Daddy's yacht on the north shore of Sydney.'

'Mate, you're a long way off. This is where I was born, and this is where I learned my way around the water. Mightn't look much, but there's plenty to do if you love the sea.' Jake picked up a rope and wrapped it around his hand ready to moor when they reached the Bay. 'You've gone soft being on the *Cote d'Azur*.'

'Hey captain, I did my time out of Darwin when I was a young bloke just like you. I know the tropics. I just can't see why you'd leave what you had in Europe to come home to this.' He lifted his hand from the helm and spread his arms wide.

'*Home* is the key word, Gus.' Jake crossed to the side of the deck and watched as they motored slowly past the small town of Karumba. A low timber bridge on a narrow neck of the river provided access to the few houses across at Second Chance Bay, but most residents of the settlement found it quicker to go across the river by boat, leaving their cars near the boat ramp at Karumba.

The wash of the boat ruffled the water and the sound of the small waves breaking on the shore behind them was louder than the quiet inboard motors.

Jake stared as they passed the large fish co-op on the riverbank just past the zinc pipeline.

'It was time to come home,' he said softly.

Home on his terms.

Jake swallowed, unsure of how he felt. McDOUGAL'S FISH CO-OP was still emblazoned on the rusty roof of the big shed. He knew at least one of the McDougal boys had stayed in town and taken over from old Bill McDougal. He'd kept in touch with a couple of local friends in the early years—those who stayed loyal to him—and they'd let him know that Bill had died a few years back. Considering the way Jake had left town, he hadn't been tempted to express his sympathy for the passing of a man who'd called him a liar and a thief.

Besides anything he'd sent—cards or flowers—would have ended up in the bin with the fish scraps if he knew the McDougal family. They were loyal and stuck together. Okay, he was sorry old man McDougal had died, but he'd been a right bastard to Jake, and he'd caused him a lot of grief in the year before he'd fled town when he was only nineteen.

Straight after high school. Straight after—

Nope, he wasn't going there.

With a shrug, Jake turned away from the view of the co-op and looked across to the other side of the river. Two jabirus picked their way along the muddy bank in the mangroves looking for food, occasionally wading into the water in their search for crabs and fish. He stared at them until the cruiser passed the docks on the portside, lost in his thoughts.

'What's the go with all the big ships?' Gus pointed to a large vessel at one of the docks, his words pulling Jake from his memories.

'Karumba is the main port up here on the Gulf,' Jake replied. 'Mining, fishing and live cattle exports are its lifeblood. Not to mention the tourism. You'll be surprised how busy it gets here in the river.'

'And you're about to make it busier with the new charter business. Showing off the crabs and crocs, and a bit of fishing on the side.'

Jake shook his head with a grin. 'And a little bit more upmarket than what they're used to, mate. I did learn a bit over in the Med. I'm planning some big trips up the coast. The best fishing in the world around here.'

'Sounds good to me. But you'll need the crew that I'm picking up to make it work.'

'Don't worry. I picked well. It was worth taking the week for the interviews.'

Gus nodded and stared ahead as the river curved in a wide arc.

'Okay, take her across to the other side when we get past the next bend in the river.' Jake headed across to the wheelhouse. 'The Bay starts a couple of hundred metres past the bend. The entrance is narrow but deep enough to get this baby into the jetty. There's a deep-water dock just near my house.' Jake rubbed his hand over his chin and hid a smile.

The house. The Jones' family mansion.

'Right, captain.' White teeth flashed again in Gus's tanned, leathery face. The older man become a good friend to Jake over the past few years and had jumped at the chance of a job as the master on one of Jake's new boats back in northern Australia.

It seemed a long time since Jake's first night in Monte Carlo, when as a raw nineteen-year-old he'd found a bar where he could afford to buy a drink—not that there were many affordable bars for a backpacker looking for a job and somewhere cheap to stay. When he'd heard the Aussie drawl at the other end of the bar, Jake had finished his beer, made his way up to the group, and watched Gus holding court.

Once he'd listened to the conversations and established that the men were all deckies like he was, he'd made himself known, and within twenty-four hours Jake had his first job on a boat out of Monte Carlo marina. Having his Master four qualification, and his marine engine driver's ticket had made him very employable, and he'd worked hard in the marina and on the boats out of Monaco for five years, before he'd bought his first boat. Jake had soon found if you were prepared to work hard, and not drink your money in the local watering holes, there was good—and fast— money to be made.

'Okay, swing her hard to port. You're almost there.'

As Gus steered the cruiser to the decrepit wooden jetty, he stared at the house ahead.

'You're kidding me, right?' Gus's eyes were wide, and Jake grinned.

The derelict house was no worse than it had been when he'd grown up here. The only difference was his mother had passed away not long after Jake had left town.

Jake had never known who his father was, and the experience of seeing Bill McDougal in action with his sons had left him with no desire to ever find out. He'd been quite happy the way things were.

Maybe if he was honest, it could have been the lack of a father figure in his life that had led him to make the wrong choices when he'd lived in Second Chance Bay. "Punching above his weight" had been the term used by Bill McDougal.

It was ironic that he'd discovered who his father was when Mum's solicitor had written to him three years after her death; his life had changed dramatically from that moment.

Jake shook his head. If he was going to spend his time back in town regretting the past and getting maudlin, he might as well turn around and head back to Europe now.

He jumped up onto the side of the boat and turned to Gus with a big grin. 'No, Gus, this is home. This is where I grew up.'

Still with sagging windows, the rusting roof, the broken gutters, and the faded paint, the house was a mess, as much a mess as it had always been—yep, he was home. It looked no worse than it had when he'd left. Maybe the jungle of weeds was a bit longer and the fence between the house and the dock had fallen over, but it was the place he wanted to be. The place he was going to make his home again.

'Welcome home, Jake,' he said softly under his breath.

Chapter Two

After *Moonshine* was tied securely to the end of the dock, and he and Gus had checked out the house, Jake lowered one of the rubber tenders from the back of the cruiser and headed across the river.

Gus had scratched his head as they walked through the house. Cobwebs formed intricate patterns, catching the last sunlight of the day. In a couple of rooms, the vines had grown through the windows and creatures had deposited their waste on the old wooden floorboards.

'You really grew up there?'

'I did.'

A frown this time. 'And you wanted to come back here? In fact, from memory, it's all you talked about over in Monaco.'

'Yep. This is home.'

Gus shook his head and his grey curls fell over his forehead. 'Mate, I know childhood memories colour our perception of things, but are you really goddamned serious about living here?'

'I'll live on one of the boats between charters until I do the old place up. This is going to be my home. Nothing that a good builder can't fix.'

'I don't just mean the house. I mean in this town.'

'Yep.' Jake's voice was clipped.

'So you're serious about basing your charter business here?'

'I am.' Jake didn't see the need to explain himself to anyone. 'You want to come on board, you're welcome. If you want to go—' He shrugged and waited for Gus's reply.

The older man stared at him intently for a long moment. 'I committed to you, Jake, and I'm in. I just wonder about the financial viability of setting up here.' Gus turned and looked at the house and Jake's gaze followed the older man's eyes. He let himself see it as someone else would.

Someone who was looking at the house without the memories that he held; the memories that had helped him through the ten years away from home.

The timber slatted boards had weathered to a dull grey, and the rusted roof was missing a couple of sheets of iron. Vines had grown over the front porch and the whole picture reminded him of an old house he'd seen on the bayou in Florida when he'd visited there on a boat-buying trip a couple of years ago. Long grass almost reached the top of the old fence that separated the house yard from the river, and he swallowed when his throat closed as he stared at the two timber posts holding the wire of the old-fashioned clothesline.

He could still see Mum there, an apron with a pocket for the pegs wrapped around her slim figure as she hung out the washing. Her black curls flying in the breeze and a perpetual smile on her face.

Jake closed his eyes as nostalgia sat heavily in his chest. This was the place he'd grown up and had had a happy childhood.

Just him and Mum.

He hadn't been able to afford to come home for her funeral. Her sister from Sydney had come up and taken care of the details and Mum had been buried in the cemetery on the other side of the river. The Jones—he had taken his mother's name— had been original settlers in Second Chance Bay in the early 1900s. He had to hold the happy memories and make a life here on them.

Jake turned to Gus and kept his voice upbeat. 'The financial prospects of a charter business aren't your worry, but rest assured you'll get paid, no matter what.'

'I'm not worried about that. I'm worried about the long-term prospects for you. You really think you can make a go of it here?'

'Not your worry.' Jake had turned to the tender at the back of the cruiser. 'Get yourself settled. Grab a couple of beers from the fridge. I'm going across the river to get us a feed of the best prawns you'll ever taste. I won't be long.'

The dock at the back of the fish cop-op was one he was very familiar with. He'd lost count of the number of times he'd tied various boats up to it over the years. From the first rowboat, he'd had when he'd been a young boy to the small inboard launch that he and the McDougal boys had fished in right through high school, to the afternoons when he'd served in the shop after school so Sally McDougal could go home and cook dinner for her family.

It was the place where he and Jenni had sat and shared their dreams.

He wondered which, if any, of the brothers was in the fish co-op today and more to the point what sort of reception he'd receive, if it was still held by the McDougals. Jake looped the rope of the tender around the post and pulled himself up the bank. The car park was empty and for a moment he paused, wondering if the co-op was still trading. The prawns weren't his reason for coming across river; he needed to see if any of the McDougal family were actually still in town, because if there was one thing his future—his success— was going to ride on, it would be their reception to his reappearance. He was sorry that old man McDougal wasn't here to see him come back to town. He was pretty sure the boys would have stayed here; he couldn't see them leaving the Bay.

Jenni was a different matter; she'd be long gone. Shame she wouldn't see that he'd made it.

A successful businessman who'd made something of his life.

The brothers—he couldn't bring himself to think about Jenni's dismissal of him—had believed their father.

Always the bad boy of Second Chance Bay, Jake had left town in a hurry.

***

Jenni McDougal stood by the window at the back of the fish co-op and dragged in a breath of fresh, clean—non-fishy—air. Her three brothers owed her big time for this; she'd only been home one day and already she'd been seconded into the fish shop, despite their promise that if she came home for her winter holiday, she'd not have to work there. Donny and Dane were out on the two boats on a week-long charter, and Matt had driven down to Normanton for a meeting with the bank.

Pah. She should have known better than to believe a word they said. After being the baby sister of three boys for the past twenty-eight years, she knew what her brothers were like. She might love them all dearly, but she'd forgotten that they'd do anything to get their own way. Eight years in the city, completing her degree and working as a casual teacher had taught her to trust again. In the classroom, the five-year-olds she taught kept their word and taught her to look at the world with fresh eyes. Trust and faith in others had come back slowly, but Jenni was still wary.

But not enough apparently. Home one day, and Jenni had fallen for the spiel of her eldest brother; hook, line, and sinker Matt had reeled her in.

'Come on, Jen. It's only for a couple of hours.' Matt had been at his most persuasive, as she'd looked up at him and folded her arms.

'No.'

'It'll save Mum having to work there before she goes off to cook at the pub.'

Jenni had wavered a tiny bit and then shaken her head. 'Hire someone. What would you have done if I hadn't been at home?'

'There's no one to hire. All the young blokes have headed off to the mines. We have enough trouble getting deckies on the charter boats now, let alone work in the shop'

'I'll do the charters anytime, but you know how much I hate working in the co-op.'

'What's the difference, sis? You don't mind handling fish on the boats. There's no difference.'

'Oh, give me a break, Matt. You can tell *you* never go out on the charters.' Jenni stood at the back door of the co-op and looked across the river to Second Chance Bay where their house was. 'There's fresh air out there, and there's nothing like the thrill of landing a big one. It's a bit different to being in and out of a fishy-smelling cool room all day, lugging ice, and serving cantankerous customers. And seeing those poor dead fish.' She shivered. 'All those fishy eyes staring at me from the display cabinet.'

'Cantankerous? I don't have cantankerous customers.' Matt shook his head.

'Well, they must all save it up for when I work there.'

Jenni had worked in the co-op when she'd been at high school and had hated every minute of it. Her father had finally given in and hired Jake Jones, much to Jenni's delight. A couple of weeks later she'd been caught out; Dad was supposed to be on a charter, but the boat had come in early. When he'd walked into the shop and spotted her sitting on the bench swinging her legs as she talked to Jake, Dad's eyes had narrowed.

'You can come back and work at the shop seeing you find it so interesting all of a sudden. There's no point me paying that boy if you're going to be hanging around.'

Jenni had flinched and shrunk back when Dad's eyes had narrowed on Jake.

'It's okay, Dad. I was just getting something for Mum.' She'd nodded and scurried away, leaving Jake to wear Dad's temper.

Jake Jones.

The boy she'd had a crush on right through high school; the boy who'd eventually shown her you couldn't trust anyone. She pushed away the memories; her plan had been to stay in town and study externally and get a job here in the local high school, but life had put paid to that. A couple of years after she'd finished school and had saved enough to leave home, Jenni headed to Brisbane and studied for her teaching degree and worked at nights in a variety of jobs.

Anything was better than staying home and working in the family fish co-op as her father had expected her to.

'Jenni?'

She jumped and stared at her brother as he looked at her, his head tipped to the side and a pleading look in his eyes. 'Please?'

'Oh, all right then. But if you're not back by lunchtime, I'm closing up early.' She jutted her chin out and glared at him, and was rewarded by a kiss on the top of her head as Matt headed back to the small office at the side of the co-op.

'Love ya, sis. It's good to have you home.'

And now here she was here again in the shop, almost as soon as she'd come back home.

But this time, she was here to stay.

All she had to do was tell her family she wasn't going back to the city.

##

Of course, Matt hadn't been back by lunchtime. Jenni had handled smelly fish, doled out kilo after kilo of frozen prawns to a constant influx of grey nomies, kept a cheery smile on her face, assured them that yes, the fish were caught locally, as well as recommending tours for those interested in going on a charter. The famous McDougal tour out to the sand island at low tide every afternoon or night—depending on the tide—was the main thing that kept their business in the black. In the winter anyway, when the grey nomies were in town. They took the groups out to the sandbar to watch the sunset, fed them marinated fish and prawns, champagne and beer, and gave each guest a glass or stubby holder imprinted with the McDougal Croc Tour logo.

She'd been so cranky with Matt, that for a brief second she'd even thought about closing up the shop at two.

When she'd rung the house at three o'clock to see if her brother was back, Mum had laughed.

'Matt won't be home till later tonight.'

'Why? What happened? Did he get a flat on that dreadful road?' The road from Karumba to Normanton was notorious for flat tyres as vehicles headed into the ditch on the side of the narrow red dirt road as they tried to avoid the big road trains.

'No, Jen. He's got a girlfriend in town. Getting some salt, I'd say.' Mum's giggle came across the phone line. 'She's a sweetheart. The new librarian at the shire library. I think our Matt's in love.'

'Salt? What on earth are you talking about, Mum?'

'Then again . . .' Mum sounded thoughtful.

Jenni could see Mum standing in the kitchen, tapping a finger on her lips.

'Then again what?'

'It could be lust.'

'Please, Mum.' Jenni rolled her eyes.

Was she seriously having this conversation with her mother?

As she stood in the cool room with stinking prawns surrounding her and with a horrid pair of yellow wellington boots on her feet, Jenni put her hand over her eyes and then quickly dropped it to her side.

Ergh. Her fingers smelled like fish guts.

'Mum, you're not losing the plot are you?'

'God, no. I'm too young for that. Although thirty years with your father—God rest his soul—was probably enough to send me troppo.'

'So what were you talking about?' Jenni leaned forward and frowned as a huge flash motor cruiser motored up the middle of the channel, a tall guy with dark brown hair standing near the edge of the deck. For a minute, it was like a blast from the past and she blinked before she spoke.

Kill the memories.

'Salt?' she said.

'Don't worry about it, sweetheart. If you don't know what salt is, I'm not the one to tell you. Ask your brothers.' There was that giggle again. 'I'm off to work now. I'll cook dinner for you before I go.'

'Thanks, Mum. See you later.' It was good to hear Mum sounding so happy, but Jenni's voice was distracted as she placed the old-fashioned phone receiver back up on the wall.

All morning Matt had bemoaned the lack of money to put into the business. The co-op building needed repairs, the cost of fuel was going up every time they set off on charters that were getting harder to fill each trip as customers looked for five-star luxury accommodation and meals on the week-long charters.

The fishing charters had been one of Dad's ideas that had worked.

Probably the only one.

Summer was a different matter; at least she'd come home in the winter and the town was alive with visitors and business was brisk.

Finally, there was a lull in the shop. There were no customers at the counter and the car park was empty so Jenni took the opportunity to step out the back to the small patch of lawn between the building and the river. Leaning back on the sun-warmed wall she inhaled deeply; the fresh cool air was pleasant after the cold air of the shop. Tipping her head back she looked up river and smiled. It was so good to be home. Since she'd left, she'd only been home once—for Dad's funeral. Her guilt at fleeing soon after school hadn't eased at all.

Not that her family had known why she'd left, although she'd always suspected that Mum had known there was more to her leaving than a burning desire to go to university.

I should have gone into acting, she thought with a grim smile.

As she stood there watching the gulls swoop over the water, the bell on the shop door tinkled. Tucking her hair back behind her ears, and picking up the heavy plastic apron she'd slipped off, she pushed open the door.

'Good afternoon, what can I—' Jenni's mouth dropped open and her world tilted. For a moment she could only stare. The apron slipped unheeded from her fingers and she took one hesitant step forward as her heart set up a tattoo of beats to rival an AC DC song. It was the man she'd seen in the motor cruiser a few minutes ago. The man she'd thought looked like Jake Jones.

It *was* Jake Jones.

Chapter Three

'J-J-Jake?

Swallowing. Jenni stopped and gripped the edge of the counter as she fought to regain her equilibrium. The cocky good looks, the same cute dimple on his chin, and the gold-flecked hazel eyes that picked up the sunshine when he was outside. The tumbling curls had gone, replaced by a sharp short haircut, but the semi-unshaven look was still there; a narrow short beard followed his jawline.

Jake Jones was still as gorgeous as ever. Jenni's heart beat harder; she put a shaking hand to her hair and then dropped it abruptly. Her knees were trembling and she fought for calm.

'That's me.' He took his eyes from her for a moment to look at the fish nestled on the ice in the glass display cabinet next to the cash register, and Jenni took a deep breath to steady herself. Bending down, she picked up the apron and slipped it over her head, and then wiped her sweaty hands on the back of her jeans.

When she looked up again, that golden gaze locked on hers so quickly, a tremor ran down her spine.

'Back for a visit?' she finally managed to splutter. 'I'm surprised to see *you* in town, Jake.'

'Me? Why would you be surprised?' He moved closer to the counter and she took a step back. Surely he wouldn't have the hide to touch her? 'I thought you'd be long gone,' he said.

'Well, I'm not as you can see.'

'I can. And a very nice picture it is too.' He grinned and she looked down at the bright yellow plastic apron. 'It'll be good to have a talk and catch up, Jenni.'

A simple request, but one she wasn't having a bar of.

'I don't think we've got anything to talk about, Jake.' She lifted her chin and kept her voice even as she stared back at him.

'I think we do, Jen.'

'Don't call me that.' The retort slammed out before she could pull it back, but he ignored it.

'I was sorry to hear about your father,' he said, those hazel eyes boring into hers.

Those words fired her up even more. 'Were you? There's no need to be polite for the sake of it. I think you of all people have a damn hide setting foot in the shop.' She folded her arms to stop them shaking. 'In fact, I think you have a hide setting foot back in town.'

'Well, sweetheart, it's a free world, so they say.'

The lazy twang of his voice sent a familiar shiver down Jenni's spine. She swallowed but Jake kept talking before she could speak.

'I am surprised to see *you* still in town. What are you doing wasting your life serving fish? What happened to your dreams?' His gaze was intense.

'Wasting my life? I'm quite happy with the life choices, *I* made, thank you.' There was no need for him to know what those choices were and that she was only here under sufferance this afternoon.

He had barely changed; his face was still boyish, but there were laughter lines around his eyes that hadn't been there before. Jake shrugged, and Jenni couldn't help raking her gaze down his lean body. His shoulders were broad and the white polo shirt with the navy blue insignia moulded a muscled chest. He put his hands on the counter and she stared at his forearms; they were tanned, sprinkled lightly with fair hair, and whipcord strong. He was too close to the counter to see his jeans, but her memory sufficed there. She swallowed again as she remembered the strong muscular thighs of his youth.

Heaven help her.

The boy she had known so well had grown into a man since she'd last seen him—almost ten years ago. The night he'd come tapping on her bedroom window, begging her to talk to him, but the events of that afternoon had been imprinted on her heart, and she'd slammed the window shut in his face.

The memory of him walking dejectedly away across the paddock to his rowboat had stayed with her for a long time.

But the memory of Jake's betrayal was one she'd never forgotten.

##

Jake cursed himself for coming to the co-op the minute he'd hit Second Chance Bay.

Bloody fool. You couldn't stay away, could you? he castigated himself silently. Although the last person he'd expected to see in the shop was Jenni. He hadn't even expected to see her in town.

He'd suspected the brothers were still around because the charters that their family had run for years were still going. He'd Googled them and also found the Facebook page for the Gulf fishing charters that had run here since he was a kid.

Of course he'd Googled; it was good business sense. You had to know the opposition when you were setting up a business. And depending on which of the brothers was running the business, he had a proposition to put to them.

He might be a fool, but old habits die hard.

It was old man McDougal he'd had the problem with, but he was gone now.

Knowing that had let Jake begin to plan to come home.

The reception he was going to receive from the town and the McDougal family was going to be interesting, but he was a big boy now and he knew he wouldn't take the shit that had been doled out to him back then.

The silence between them was broken only by the hum of the freezers at the side of the shop, and the constant vibration of the cool room door behind the counter. Jake walked across to the large glass-fronted fridge at the side of the store where the fresh prawns had been kept when he had worked here in his late teens. He looked around, raising his eyebrows, surprised at the state of the equipment. The fridge was rusted along the bottom and the glass door was scratched, and it was hard to see what seafood was behind the glass door. The shop looked uncared for— and old. Even the smell of the seafood was stale; the fresh clean smell of salt was overlaid by the smell of old fish.

He turned back to the counter. 'Do you have any fresh king prawns?'

Jenni's eyes widened. She had been expecting to continue their conversation.

'Um, yes. There's some in the cool room. How many do you want?' Her voice was as chilly as the ice in the front cabinet.

'A couple of kilos.' He gestured to the cool room. 'Are they fresh?'

'Of course, they are.' She turned with a flourish and opened the door of the cool room. Jake couldn't help admiring the cute bottom in the snug-fitting jeans as she disappeared into the depths. He waited until she came out and placed two plastic bags of prawns on the newspaper on the counter.

'Will that be all?' Jenni folded her arms as she waited for his reply. Her light brown hair was still tipped by fine blonde streaks where the sun had lightened it. Her complexion was pale but flawless— he smiled to himself as he remembered her insistence on always wearing a hat the minute she'd stepped outside. Her green eyes were wide as she stared at him waiting for him to answer.

'I guess it will be for today.'

Jenni's movements were deft as she quickly wrapped the plastic bags in newspaper, and put them into another white plastic bag. 'That will be forty dollars please.'

Her voice was impersonal as though he was a stranger.

Jake pulled out his Amex business card and passed it over but she shook her head and pointed to a sign next to the cash register.

Cash only. No EFTPOS.

Digging into his wallet, he pulled out a fifty-dollar note. Jenni's eyes were downcast and she didn't meet his gaze as she took the money and rang up the sale.

'Thank you,' he said as she handed him the change. Her fingers brushed against his and she pulled her hand back as though she'd burned her fingers.

He stood there for a moment and she finally lifted her eyes to his.

'I was sorry to hear of your mother's passing, Jake.'

'Thanks.' He nodded as he took the bags from the counter. 'I guess I'll be seeing you around. Are the boys still here?'

'They are.' As she replied her eyes dropped to the Moonshine Charter insignia on his polo shirt and her cheek coloured as her lips tightened. 'Moonshine?' she said. 'You're working for the new charter company?'

He couldn't help himself as he turned for the door.

'No, Jen. I *am* Moonshine. It's my company.'

Chapter Four

Jenni was quiet as she pushed open the front door of the house she had grown up in at Second Chance Bay. As she'd crossed the river, she leaned forward and stared up river to where the sleek white cruiser was moored at the dilapidated jetty of the Jones' house. Her mood was black; Matt hadn't shown up and after she'd cleared the till, put the cash in the white bank bag and secured it in her backback. Jenni had pulled down the blind on the front door of the shop. The mechanism at the top had snapped and the torn and tattered blind had fallen to the floor. She'd stepped over it, and locked the shop door behind her.

Honestly, what was Matt doing with the family business? She'd seen the shop through Jake's eyes as he'd looked around and embarrassment had heated her face as she'd taken it all in anew.

Embarrassment, as well as a riot of feelings that had surged through her from the moment he'd walked into the shop. Such a storm of feelings, she was going to have a serious rethink of her plans, if Jake Jones was moving back to town.

Her thoughts were tumultuous, tripping over each other, and exposing feelings that she'd hidden away for a long time. The feelings that had stopped her from having any successful relationships at university, and when she'd started work at her first school. Every time she went on a date, she compared the guy to Jake, and the bottom line was—no one ever measured up. She knew her brothers were the same. In their thirties—well Donny was almost there—and not a serious relationship to be seen. The attitude of their father had probably talked them out of ever settling down and having their own family.

It was crazy, but after so many failed attempts at relationships, Jenni had decided to focus on her teaching career, and forget about meeting anyone. If it happened one day, well and good; if it didn't she'd be a career teacher and work her way up to a promotion position.

The plans had been there, but a permanent job hadn't eventuated. There were too many graduates looking for jobs in the city, and finally, she realised if she wanted a job, she would have to go bush.

But she hadn't told her family about the job yet. That was going to be a surprise for Mum.

Her stomach was still churning and her hands shaking as she closed the front door of the McDougal family house on the river. Even though they were in the tropics, the wind that came off the water in winter could be cool at night. Her hands were red and chapped from being in ice all day and she didn't think she'd ever get the smell of the fish from her fingers.

As the door clicked shut Matt's voice came down the hall. 'Is that you, Mum? Where did you put my good denim jeans? I need them to go out to the poker game with the boys at the pub.'

Jen pulled off her backpack and put it on the table inside the door as her eldest brother strolled down the hallway.

'Oh hi, Jen. I thought you were Mum home for her break.'

'Don't you 'hi Jen' me, you louse.' The temper that had been building in her chest ever since Jake Jones had pushed open the door of the fish shop burst out in one angry torrent.

'How dare you leave me in the shop all day? I had things to do and a Skype meeting with the education board that I had to cancel. I'll never work there for you again! Is that clear? I'm over it, Matt I've been home less than twenty-four hours, and I've spent nine of them in the stinking fish co-op.' Jenni's voice got louder as she let out her feelings.

'Whoa, calm down.' Matt held his hands up. 'I'm really sorry. I've just got back. I'm sorry you had to spend the day there, but I got tied up, honestly, sis.'

'Yeah, with a woman, Mum reckons.' Jen put her hands on her hips. 'And just how old are you, Matthew McDougal? Mum is still washing and ironing for you and putting your clothes away?' Once she'd started Jenni couldn't stop. 'I'm sure I'm adopted. Between the behaviour of the three of you and the way Dad treated Mum—God rest his soul— there is no way I'm related to any of you. No wonder poor Mum—'

Her oldest brother's hands descended on her shoulders and his voice was quiet. 'Jenni. Just calm down. I'm sorry. I should've rung you but the solicitor called me and he managed to squeeze me in. I was all afternoon in his office.'

Jenni sniffed and looked at him suspiciously. 'Mum said it was something to do with salt.'

Matt wrinkled his forehead for a moment and then he burst out laughing. 'I can assure you I had no time for any 'salt'. Look I'm really sorry I stuffed up your day, but why are you so upset? It's not like you at all, sweets. I've never heard you yell before. Is that what school teaching has taught you?' His grin was wide as he stared down at her affectionately

Jenni ducked from beneath his hands and pushed past him. She walked down the hallway, not able to help herself from stomping on the bare wooden floorboards. It was a satisfying sound and one that she'd used a lot when she was angry with their father in her teens. Pulling out the old kitchen chair, she flopped onto it. 'Put the kettle on and I might forgive you.' She ran her hands over the red laminate of the kitchen table. Nothing had changed in this room since she was a child. It just looked a bit older and worn these days.

Matt shot her a look and walked over to the stove and picked up the ceramic kettle off the hob before crossing to the sink and filling it. 'Tea or coffee?'

'Coffee, please.' Jenni sat back and looked around. Mum had always done her best to keep the house nice, but before Dad died, any spare money had always gone back into the business. By the look of the fish co-op—she hadn't seen any of the charter boats yet—she wondered how much money there was to go into the business—or the family house— these days.

'The place looks run down,' she said.

Matt nodded. 'There's not a lot of spare cash these days, sis. The house is the last on the list. We could really do with a new boat, especially with the new company coming into town. What Mum earns goes towards the rates and the upkeep of the old place, but it's never enough.'

Regret shot through Jenni. It was hard that Mum had to keep working. She'd worked in the shop when Dad had been alive, and now she was working at the pub, cooking for the tourists.

She screwed up her nose as Matt leaned back against the sink and looked at her. 'Money's tight, but we do what we can.'

'Did you say you were going to a poker game?' Jenni asked with a frown.

'Yeah, there's a few deckies in town who like a game. We play every Monday night.'

'For money?' Jenni couldn't help the suspicious note that crept into her voice.

His lips were set in a straight line. 'No, Jen. Not for money. You don't need to worry. I didn't inherit Dad's gambling habits.'

'Sorry.' She propped her chin in her hand as Matt turned and lit the gas. 'I noticed how old the shop was looking too.'

'It's been a very quiet season. But now the grey nomies have started to arrive, business at the shop and on the charters will pick up. It always does. We'll be okay.'

The kettle came to the boil quickly on the gas flame and Matt filled two mugs with instant coffee and poured the hot water in before he crossed to the old rusted Kelvinator fridge to get the milk out.

'Ta.' Jenni nodded her thanks as he put the mug in front of her. He sat beside her and gestured over to the stove.

'Mum's left a casserole in the oven. She always cooks for whoever is home before she goes to work.' To his credit, he did look a bit sheepish.

'Really, Matt? Mum's still got the three of you at home.' She shook her head. 'How old are you? Donny will be thirty next birthday, and you and Dane are already in your thirties. And you're all still home and poor Mum is cooking, cleaning and washing for you? It's a bit rough.'

'Mum doesn't mind. She said she likes having the company. A couple of times we talked about moving out and she didn't like the idea. Although lately—

Matt paused and scratched his chin.

'Lately what?' Jenni picked up her mug and took a sip.' Her hands had finally stopped shaking, and calm had returned. If anything she was cross with herself for her overreaction to Jake, and her outburst with Matt.

Although he could have rung me to say he was going to be late.

'She has been getting out and about a lot more in the past few months. She never used to go anywhere much at all.'

'Doing what?' Jenni frowned. Mum had always been too busy for the social events in town.

'She goes to the different clubs at the pub through the week. She's been playing darts, and she's joined the historical society. The other night she was talking about taking a bus trip across the Savannah Way all the way to Broome.'

'Really? Good on her.'

Matt shook his head. 'The problem is I don't know if we can afford it.'

Jenni stared at him in disbelief. 'Are you for real, Matthew? After what Mum has done for you, you can't even help her out with a holiday? And she's cooking at the pub at nights too?'

'Look, Jenni. You've been away. You don't know how tight we are. Insurance costs for the boats and the cost of fuel have skyrocketed over the past few years. Between charters, Dane and Donny work over on the ships, while I man the shop.' Matt's dark brows lowered in a frown. 'And now our biggest worry is the rumour that the new charter business will start up on the river this season.'

Jenni put her mug down with a thump. 'That rumour appeared in the shop this afternoon.'

'What?' Matt's eyes were wide and he put his mug down and leaned forward. 'You mean they're here in town already? I haven't seen any ads up on the notice boards yet.

'Jake Jones is back in town. On one of the flashest boats I've seen here for a long time. I don't think it's the type of business where they'll be putting photocopied black and white ads up in the caravan parks.'

'He's come back to the Bay to work?'

'No. It's *his* company. Or so he told me this afternoon. And by the look of the boat, and the swish shirt and logo, it's going to make it hard for us.'

Matt's smile stunned her. 'That's great. I'm really pleased he's made a success of his life. He always was a good guy.'

A good guy?

'And it doesn't bother you that he's come back to town to take a share of the tourist trade?'

'No. If it has to happen, I think it's great that it's Jake. At least it's someone we know and we can work with him. Like I said he was always a decent guy.'

'You've got a very short memory. What about what he did to us? It doesn't bother you how he left town?'

Matt stared at her over the rim of his coffee mug and his gaze was level. 'I think Dad can take a lot of the blame for what happened and the way you reacted.'

'Jake *stole* from us, Matt. We trusted him. Dad gave him a job, and he *stole* from the very hand that fed him.'

She didn't even mention that Jake's deception had broken her heart. He hadn't been the person she'd thought he was. But her brother wasn't going to let it go.

'I always believed if Jake took that money, he had very good reason to. His mother did it tough, and he adored her—'

Jenni snorted. 'Yes. So much that he didn't even come home from Europe for her funeral.'

'Don't be so judgmental. I know he broke your heart when he took off, but I'm sure he had his reasons for not coming home.'

'He didn't break my heart.' Jenni picked up her mug and stood. 'I'm going to have a shower. I smell like fish.'

'Jen?' Matt's voice was soft. 'Don't be hard on Jake. Give him a chance.'

Jenni stood in the kitchen and stared long and hard at her brother before she shook his head. He'd always been the soft one of the four kids. The eldest, but he'd provided a good role model for being calm, and holding the legendary McDougal temper under control.

Although rather than emulating her big brother's behaviour, it was the memory of Dad's red face and raised hand that helped Jenni control hers when she felt it building. Genes were strong, but not strong enough to make her cruel.

And she knew her brothers were the same. All three of them.

'No, Matt. I won't. He let me down. It was obviously in his character, and he won't have changed. I'm just surprised that you're not more upset about him coming to town. It's going to impact on our business.'

'*Our* business?' Matt fired up for a change and Jenni took a step back. 'First time I've ever heard you interested in *our* business.'

'Oh, go take a flying leap.' Jenni threw her mug in the sink and it clattered against the metal. Matt muttered something under his breath as she walked out, but she didn't go back to hear what he said.

'And Jen?' Matt called after her. 'Do you really want to know what 'salt' is?

She poked her head back around the door. 'Yes, what was Mum on about?'

His grin was wicked. 'Sex at lunchtime.'

Jenni giggled as she turned for the hallway.

'*Oh, Mum!*' she thought.

Chapter Five

Jake leaned on the wheelhouse on the top deck and watched the moon rise. The high-pitched whine of the osprey across the river rose to a wavering squeal as another osprey approached the nest. He watched the interaction until the second bird flew away. He lifted his beer and took a long draught.

Being back home was strange.

Gus had gone down to the cabin for an early night, as he had a six a.m. start to meet the helicopter. Jake had opted to stay up on deck for a while, and he was using the time to try to get his thoughts in order. Sitting on the leather bench seat on the deck of his luxurious charter boat, and looking back at the house that he'd grown up in was a strange feeling. It was as though his past and current lives were running in parallel. If he closed his eyes, the sounds were the same as the nights he and the McDougal brothers had gone fishing around the point in the small launch that Dane had bought and done up. They'd always been complacent about crocodiles, and now as an adult, Jake shook his head, thinking how lucky they'd been as they'd spent so much time on the water. He was the same age as Donny McDougal, and it was Donny who'd brought him home from school to play on their first day in kindergarten.

Jake could still remember an overheard comment at a school swimming carnival one summer when Sally McDougal had cheered for him in a race.

Something like *'that Jones boy isn't good enough for the McDougal family.'*

Mum had heard it too, and he could still remember the pride on her face when he'd won his first place ribbon, but he could also remember the hurt that was in her eyes when the comment had been made in the silence before the applause for the winners. Old Mrs Jackson from the bakery had a loud voice.

But he'd never felt second best with the McDougal family. From Sally or the three boys. He'd been welcome in their home and was almost a fourth son in the family right through primary and high school. Hell, there'd even been a spare bed for him in Donny's room.

And Jenni. He'd never felt second best with her either. He pushed her from his thoughts. Last he'd heard—he'd kept in touch with the news before Mum had passed away—Jenni had moved to Brisbane.

He'd assumed that she would have been married, and had a couple of kids by now.

If Jake had known she was living here at Second Chance Bay and working in the family business at Karumba, he might have reconsidered setting up his business here.

It was Jenni whose opinion had mattered the most. It always had. The comments of the townspeople, and the judgment passed on him there he could handle. Although he did know that was why he'd come back to town, to prove to the critics that he'd made it.

Stupid really.

Probably most of those who had judged him at the time were long gone. And ironically the one person he wanted to prove himself to was the one who could never know the truth. He wouldn't do that to Jenni.

A light flickered across the shore at the wharf up from the pub. As he sat there, the low putt-putt of an outboard motor reached him.

'Ahoy, there. Anyone on board?'

With a grin, Jake put his beer on the table and walked to the back of the boat.

'Sure is, but don't you go scratching my baby with that heap of shit you call a boat.'

Matt McDougal stepped from the dock onto the back of Jake's boat. He looked around appreciatively and whistled before he held out his hand. 'Welcome home, Jonesy boy.'

Jake looked at Matt's hand for a moment before he took it. Matt's grip was firm, and even in the shadowed moonlight, Jake could see his grin was wide.

And welcoming.

Some of the heaviness that had been in his chest all day lifted.

'Wanna beer?' he asked.

'I thought you'd never offer.' Matt followed him up to the top deck and looked around while Jake pulled a beer from the deck fridge and handed it to him.

Matt shook his head as his gaze travelled slowly over the top deck of the boat. 'You've come a long way, mate. Jenni tells me you're our new opposition in the Gulf.'

'Maybe not so much opposition.' Jake nodded. 'I was going to come and see you guys tomorrow. Are you all still in the business?'

'We are. Dane and Donny are out on charters this week. Donny's round the west of Darwin, and Dane's up near Weipa. And yes, it'll be good to chat. We'll be picking your brains.' Matt sat back and looked at Jake. 'You've done well for yourself, mate. I'm really happy for you.'

'I appreciate your words, and your welcome, much more than you'll ever know, Matt.'

Even though Jake was Donny's age, he and Matt had formed a close friendship in their teens.

'Don't expect it from all of us. Mum'll be fine and the boys will come around. Jenni's the one who holds the grudge.' Matt looked at him curiously. 'You know even though it was my father, I never believed what he said. Or if there was any truth in it, I knew you would have had a damn good reason.'

Jake shook his head. 'It's not something I'm going to talk about, mate. It's not a time of my life I like to remember, but a lot of years have gone by, and everything's changed. For all of us.'

Matt laughed. 'Maybe for you, but not so much for us, Jonesy.'

'I was surprised to see Jenni here. She's working in the business? I never thought she would.' Jake popped the top of his beer.

'Oh hell, no. I'm in the bad books because she was filling in for me for a couple of hours today, and I got held up in Normanton. She ended up working in the fish shop all day. She only arrived home from Brisbane last night.'

'So she's only visiting?'

'Yeah. She doesn't come home much. She left town a while after you did.'

'Husband and kids?' Jake kept his voice casual.

'Nah, she's a teacher and a career person through and through. She reckons she loves it, but Mum worries about her. Reckons she's not happy living away, but that's mothers for you.' He put his beer down. 'I'm sorry, mate, that was insensitive. I went to your Mum's funeral.'

'Thanks. I appreciate that. I knew you would. I didn't have the money for the airfare back from Europe. She lost her battle with breast cancer when I was still a lowly deckie. I talked to Mum every day she was in hospital in Normanton, and I know she understood. But it was still really tough, not being here for her.'

'Yeah, it would have been. She told me you used to ring her every night.'

Jake lifted his head. 'You visited her in hospital?'

Matt nodded. 'Mum and I used to take it in turns.'

Jake shook his head as his throat tightened. 'And you drove all the way to Normanton to see her? She never said.'

'Of course we did. I guess she didn't want to bring up the McDougal name to you.' Matt looked away. 'Sad thing that, when there's bad feeling between good people.'

Jake ignored the lump that had formed in his throat, but in that moment, he knew he'd been right to come home. He cleared his throat and took a swig of beer. 'I'm going to do the old place up and move in.'

'That'll take a while.'

'It will, but I'm going to settle here. I'm home now.'

'For good?'

Yep. For good.'

Matt lifted his bottle and clinked it against Jake's. 'In that case, welcome home again. There's going to be a lot of people happy to see you here. Your business is going to be good for the Bay.'

A lot of people? He knew one who wouldn't be happy.

But Jake didn't put what he was thinking into words.

Chapter Six

A week went by before Jenni saw Jake Jones again. Her temper had been short and her mood irritable when she thought about Jake being back in town. What gods were laughing down at her? Ten years, and they'd hit town in the same week?

She'd managed to—almost, anyway—forget him over the past few years, and now he was back on her radar she couldn't stop herself thinking about him.

Seeing Jake again brought what had happened slamming back into her thoughts, and she wasn't happy. Her life had been settled and she was on the path to doing what she wanted to. And she had been happy doing it. She'd been happy about coming home, but now his presence had tainted that.

Tainted. That was exactly the word. What Jake had done before he'd left town had tainted everything.

Jenni spent the past week on tenterhooks, sure she'd run into him somewhere in the small town, but he'd kept a low profile. Or maybe it was because she didn't leave the house much. The fancy boat had passed the house a couple of times as it purred smoothly up the river, but she'd ignored it.

On Friday afternoon, Mum had raised her eyebrows. 'Haven't you got something nice to do, love?' she asked as she tried to fill the kettle while Jenni washed up. 'It's lovely to have you home, sweetheart, but you need to get out of the house. Surely there's someone you want to catch up with? Have a coffee with some of the girls, maybe? Go for a run? Do you still jog and do those triathlon things?' Mum's eyes had narrowed. 'You're still too thin. I'll have to fatten you up a bit.'

Jenni shook her head. 'I still run to keep fit, but no competitions lately. I've been too busy with school stuff. I don't think any of my friends stayed in town. They've all moved away.' The one person she'd spent most of her time within the last two years of school was the one person she had no desire to catch up with.

'Why don't you go down to the dock and wait for your brothers? Matt called a few minutes ago and said they've radioed in. They'll be coming through the heads any time now. They'll both be pleased to see you.'

'I will. I thought they'd be later than this.' Jenni drained the sink and wiped her hands, hiding a smile when a look of relief crossed Mum's face. She knew Mum hated anyone else in her domain. 'I can't wait to see the boys. It's over two years since I last saw them.'

'Well, get your skates on because they'll dock in about fifteen minutes. Tell them I've got the night off. I'm just about to put a roast on so we can all have dinner together.' Mum blinked a tear away. 'It's the first time you've all been home together since your dad went.'

Jenni crossed the room and put her arms around her mother. 'I'm sorry, Mum. I've been slack.' She bit her lip as she hugged Mum close and decided to break her news. 'But I've got some news. I was going to make it a surprise when the truck arrived.'

'Truck?' Mum looked up at her, a frown creasing her brow. 'What truck?'

'The truck with all my stuff in it. I've given up my apartment in Brisbane and everything's on the way home. I've got two terms at Second Chance Bay High School in the English department.'

'Oh, my goodness!'

Jenni smiled as her mother let her go and jumped up and down on the spot, before grabbing her in another huge hug. 'Oh, my stars, that is awesome.'

'I thought you'd be happy.'

'I am but the timing is a bit hard. I've got some news too.' Mum stepped back and looked at her and her smile faltered.

'News?'

'Yes. I'm going away too. But at least you'll be here to look after your brothers,'

Jenni put her hands up. 'Whoa . . . let's backtrack a little here. First off where are you going?'

'I'm going to Broome with . . . Rick.'

'Rick from the pub?'

'Yes, he's opening a pub over in Broome too, and he invited me to go for a bit of a holiday with him.' Mum's face flushed.

'You cheeky thing. Are you seeing him?'

Her mother folded her arms. 'Yes, I see him every night when I cook at the pub.'

'You know what I mean.'

The blush deepened. 'Yes, I guess you could say we're "seeing" each other.' Her mother's forehead creased in a frown. 'Do you mind, love? The boys are okay with it. They like Rick. Her cheeks flushed. 'I—um—sometimes stay the night at his place.'

Even as surprise coursed through Jenni, she shook her head. 'Of course I don't mind, you silly thing. You deserve to be happy, Mum. It's a long time since Dad went.' She doubted that Mum had been happy before he went, but that had never been talked about.

'So yes, I'm going away for a while. Rick wants me to stay over there for six months, and help get the pub bistro set up.'

'And he'll be there too?' Jenni nudged her mother with a cheeky smile.

'Yes, he will.' Mum cleared her throat. 'And now that you're home, it solves my biggest problem. I was worried who was going to look after the boys.'

'Mum!' Jenni put her hands on her hips and her voice was a splutter of disbelief. 'If you think I'm going to look after three grown men and tell them where their jeans are and serve their Weetbix out for them each morning, they are going to be very disappointed. Very, very disappointed.'

'I know I've spoiled them.' Despite her words, Mum's smile was still wide. 'It hasn't hurt them.'

'Spoiled them? I pity the poor women they end up with. If they ever do get married. Because you know what, Mum? If you keep making it so good at home, they are going to turn into three crusty old bachelors and stay here forever. It will do them good to look after themselves while you're away. I'm really happy that you're doing it. For your sake too.' She shot a sidelong glance at her mother. 'And I like Rick too. He's a good man. I always knew he fancied you.'

'Oh, get away with you.' Mum picked up the vacuum cleaner again but she was smiling. 'Get over to the dock or you'll miss the boats coming in. Apparently, they've had good trips and they're loaded up with fish and happy guests.'

'That's what we want to hear. Return customers. Matt said it's been quiet.'

'It has, but we can talk about that later when you're all home for dinner. Now get yourself off to the boats!'

'Yes, Mum!' Jenni hurried down to her room— the room that was the same as when she'd left. Her favourite childhood books were still in the shelf at the head of the bed, and her bride doll was in pride of place on the chair beneath the window. How many nights had she lain in bed and dreamed of her own white wedding? Jenni gave a huff of disgust and pulled out a pair of long cotton pants and a clean T-shirt. It would be cool down on the dock if the wind blew up.

***

Jake and Matt sat on the fence near the public boat ramp where the charter boats moored offshore, watching the activity on the water as they waited for the two McDougal boats to come home.

'Mosquito fleet's starting to come in.' Matt nodded to the continuous fleet of ten-foot tinnies that were heading back into the river mouth. A procession of four-wheel drive vehicles grew longer as the drivers backed them down the ramp as they took turns to retrieve their boats.

'I'd forgotten that term,' Jake said with a laugh. 'All the retired blokes who go out each morning to catch a feed. There mustn't be many fish out there today. They're coming in early.'

'Nah. There's always fish.' Matt glanced down at his watch. 'It's almost beer o'clock. The happy hour groups will be starting to gather in the caravan park soon. The fishermen will just have time to clean their catch, and then pull up a chair and a beer. '

'Look at us.' Jake laughed as Matt stared out into the Gulf. 'Can you remember when we were kids and heading past this spot in the launch? We used to laugh at the old blokes sitting here watching the boats come in.'

'We're just a couple of *older* blokes now, mate. Not too old.' Matt pointed past the channel markers a couple of kilometres past the river mouth. 'Here comes Donny now.'

Jake narrowed his eyes and nodded as he made out the shape of the boat familiar to him from his teenage years. The *Sally M* had been an old boat then, but she still had class. At thirty-three metres, and sleeping thirty- four with private en suite facilities for each cabin, she was a grand old lady. When she was built she'd been one of the largest charter boats in Queensland. He'd helped the McDougal boys—and Jenni—clean her between trips and earned himself some pocket money. He was looking forward to stepping onboard and running his fingers over the beautifully polished timber inside the saloon. Even though he'd skippered some beautiful boats in Europe, they'd all been slick and modern; the *Sally M* was stylish, but he did notice she looked a bit rundown.

'It'll help you buy some fishing gear, son,' old Bill McDougal had said when he'd offered him the job. Jake had agreed but every cent had gone to Mum. Money had been short in the old house on the river.

Jake shut down the line of thought. If he let himself dwell on past events, it sat in his chest like a stone.

Am I crazy to have come back here?

No matter how many friends he'd made in the Mediterranean, how many charters he'd skippered, or how much money he'd made, happiness had eluded him there.

He sat back and watched as the *Sally M* approached the dock. Sitting here bare-footed in the sun, in his old cut-off denim shorts and a plain white T-shirt, contentment filled Jake and he began to think he'd made the right move, no matter what his doubts were. He'd shed the white linen shorts and the polo shirt with the company logo because there was no one to impress today. He stared over the water; the only person he wanted to impress would probably prefer the old Jake anyway.

Or no Jake.

'Who's minding the shop?'

The very person he'd been thinking about walked up and stood behind her brother. Jenni gave Jake a cool nod and then turned to Matt with a smile. 'You playing hooky again, Matthew?'

'No. Maisie from the caravan park is minding the shop while I help unload the fish. Donny said they've got a huge catch on board. How do you fancy helping us freeze some of it down later? I've got a flash new cryovac machine.'

'Ergh. No thank you.' Jenni tilted her head to the side and chuckled. 'Not the same Maisie from Melbourne who lived in Toorak Lane every winter when we were growing up? Maisie with the blue rinse?'

'The very same,' Matt replied. 'But the years have moved on and she's moved sites over the past couple of winters.'

Jenni's peal of laughter warmed Jake's heart, but he clenched his hands as he looked up at her.

'Tell me she hasn't moved to Dunrootin Lane?' she asked with a pretty smile, a smile that made Jake's heart speed up.

'So you haven't forgotten what they used to name the streets in the caravan park?' Matt looked at his sister with a frown. 'That's good because you've been gone way too long, Jen.'

'Well, I'm back now, and no, I haven't forgotten.' she said quietly as she kicked at a stone and avoided Jake's gaze. 'I'm going to wait down on the boat ramp. It's warmer down there.'

Jake tried not to stare as Jenni walked down the concrete ramp across from where they were sitting. She was still slim and lithe and the sun glinted on her hair that reached halfway down her back. Her shoulders were straight and she carried herself confidently. While her back was turned to him, he drank in his fill.

Matt's low voice pulled him from his need. 'That was interesting.'

'What?'

'The way Jenni said she was home now. Did you get the impression that she meant she was home, rather than just visiting?'

'Sorry, I wasn't paying much attention.' Jake pointed to the boat that was almost in front of them. 'She's still a beautiful boat.'

'A bit long in the tooth, and the upkeep costs are getting worse by the year, but yes, she's a beauty.'

'Do you ever go out on charters?' Jake turned back to Matt because while ever he was looking at the approaching boat, Jenni was in his line of sight.

'No. Would you believe the one time I went I got seasick? Not a good look for a skipper. So, I get to run the land part of the business. The bookings, the finances, the orders and the fish and prawn sales side of things.'

'So, you get the worry without all the fun?' Jake cut straight to the chase.

'Good to talk to someone who understands. The rest of the family reckons I'm a whinger.' Matt ran his hand through his tousled curls. The wind had picked up and as Jake looked back at Jenni, she was standing on her tiptoes, holding her hair with one hand. From where he was sitting, it was like looking at the eighteen-year-old girl he'd fallen in love with. She looked no different as she stood there, obviously excited about seeing her brothers.

'A whinger?' He turned his attention back to Matt. 'In what way?'

Matt sighed. 'Because I'm always on about money, Donny reckons I'm a tight arse, but the only outgoing money he sees is when he fills the diesel tanks up.'

Jake sat quietly for a minute. 'If I can I'd like to help. I know my leaving was . . . difficult . . . but I'd like to help out if I can.'

Matt's voice sparked with interest. 'In what way, mate? How can you help our business?'

'Well the *Sally M,* and also, the *Elsie*'—the other boat had been named after the matriarch of the family when Bill McDougal had started the charter business back in the eighties— 'are much bigger than my two boats. I'm thinking of an arrangement where we combine charters and you provide the mother ship, and my boats can go out deep and wide for the game fishing.'

'It could work. But I'd have to get the others to agree.' Matt held Jake's gaze steadily. 'And I'll be honest with you. You might not get the same welcome—or enthusiasm— from Dane and Donny. But I'll work on them.'

'Or Jenni,' Jake said glumly.

'You've still got it bad for her, haven't you? Even after all these years?'

'Yeah, you'd think not seeing her for so long would have cured me, wouldn't you?'

'Not to mention all those hot French chicks.'

Jake laughed. 'I was a dull boy over there, all work and no play.'

'No play?' Matt asked, his grin wide. 'None at all?'

'Well, maybe a little.'

Sometimes he'd tried to get Jenni out of his head. How long did it take to fall out of love with somebody? The old maxim, they were meant for each other had stayed active way too long. Part of his reason for coming home was to get Jenni McDougal out of his system.

To come back to the Bay, and live here without her. Settle down and accept she was gone from here and gone from his life. And what did he come home to? Jenni in town, and the same feelings surging back.

Bloody ridiculous.

Ten years.

One look at her, and Jake was right back where he'd been when her father ran him out of town.

In love and not able to do a thing about it.

There was only one answer. Immerse himself in work here like he had overseas.

But the little voice inside niggled at him.

Maybe you can change her mind.

Maybe he could show her the man he was without her knowing the truth of ten years ago?

***

Jenni stood on the boat ramp, waiting for the boats. She stood up and down on her tiptoes and grabbed for her hair again as another big gust of wind lifted it. She was conscious of Jake sitting on the fence not far behind her.

A strange feeling gripped her. Seeing him out of the swish charter boat uniform, and back in his old clothes, it was as though her old Jake was back with her.

Scrap that, not *her* Jake. No matter how hard she'd tried over the past week, he had stayed in her thoughts, and she knew she had to do something about it.

If she hadn't signed the contact with the education board for the two terms of work at the local high school, she would have gone.

Fled town like Jake had.

Her emotions were in turmoil. When she'd crossed the road to the boat ramp and spotted him sitting beside Matt, her fingertips had tingled, and her heart had sped up. She'd stood behind them for a moment, watching the wind ruffle Jake's hair, and feasted her eyes on the broad back beneath the snug fitting T-shirt. No matter what she knew about Jake Jones, her body wouldn't stop the traitorous reaction. After a couple of minutes Jenni had swallowed and walked across to them.

Moving down to the boat ramp had been a stupid move because Jake was behind her now, and she could feel his eyes on her. Maybe if they'd had closure when he'd fled town, maybe if they'd had a conversation, she wouldn't feel like this.

There'd never been any closure. One minute, they'd been inseparable, and then the next minute he'd gone.

Her family had been shocked by his actions, but Dad had been hard the afternoon he'd dropped the bombshell.

'Jake stole from us, Jen love,' he'd said the afternoon he came looking for Jenni. She'd been down at the boat ramp, where she was standing now as the memories bombarded her.

'I never trusted him,' Dad went on. 'He fitted too easily into our family, and he thought he was one of us. Blood always tells, and none of the Jones' family was ever any good. I was a fool to take the boy in and trust him.'

'What? What did he do?' Jenni's world had shifted in that moment.

Even as she thought of it ten years later, her breath hitched and her stomach churned as her father stared at her, his eyes hard.

'He's been taking some of the takings from the fish shop very day. Two thousand dollars all up. I've been watching him. I thought our till was down a bit so I tallied up the takings. I caught him at it today.'

Jenni had shaken her head as she stared up at her father. 'No. I don't believe it. Jake would never do that.'

'Well, you have to, love. He's admitted it.'

'I want to go and talk to him.' She'd pulled away from her father's grip as his fingers had circled her wrist. 'Now.'

'You can't. He's leaving.'

'Leaving?' Confusion ran rampant through her as Jenni had put her hand to her stomach, thinking she was going to be sick.

'The sergeant gave him a warning and he's driving him to Normanton tonight. I told him if he left town, I wouldn't press charges.'

'What about the money?' Jenni had barely been able to get the words out.

'I let him keep it. Maybe it'll give the boy a start.' His voice was gruff and Jenni stared at her father. Dad never gave anything to anyone; it was a good thing to do in a horrid situation to help Jake out. A turmoil of thoughts had whizzed around her head and finally disappointment and disgust had settled in her chest.

To this day, Jenni couldn't reconcile the Jake she'd known—and loved—with a man who would steal from her family, and then leave town with the proceeds.

Matt had always refused to believe that Jake was guilty, and he and Dad had had a strained relationship until the day their father had died.

Jenni glanced behind her. Matt and Jake were deep in conversation, as thick as they'd always been. A ripple of doubt, with a smidgeon of guilt thrown into the mix, ran through her. Matt had stayed loyal to Jake the whole time, and welcomed him back to town.

Why had Jake left town?

Because he was guilty.

That was the only explanation for him leaving so suddenly.

Chapter Seven

Donny came in first, and the horn of the *Sally M* tooted when he spotted Jenni on the concrete ramp. She ran across the soft sand and around to the dock where he was berthing the large vessel.

'Jen!' Once the ropes were secured Donny jumped over the side of the boat and hugged her. 'Welcome home, sis. It's about time you came to visit.'

She landed a kiss on her brother's unshaven cheek. 'You look like a hobo, Donny.'

'We've been busy catching fish. Just as well you're home; we'll need a hand to clean them all.'

Jenni pulled a face at him, and stood with her arm linked through his as their older brother, Dane, brought the second boat in.

It took an hour for the guests to disembark, and Jenni smiled as her brothers handed out large polystyrene boxes of fish to the guests. Contrary to Donny's words, she knew the fish would have been cleaned and then frozen down in the big freezers on the boats, ready for the guests to take their catches back to the southern states.

Matt came over and waited as a small crane lifted off the last big boxes of fresh fish, ready to go the shop.

'Just as well there's a crowd in town,' he said.

'A bit too much of a crowd,' Donny murmured, looking back to where Jake was sitting on the fence.

Jenni stared across to where Donny was looking. She wasn't alone in her opinion of Jake Jones coming back to town.

##

Three hours later, the atmosphere in the McDougal kitchen was noisy and happy. Donny and Dane had showered and shaved; Mum bustled about serving up a baked dinner, a satisfied expression on her face as the conversation between her four children became lively.

'I'll give you a hand, Mum.' Jenni walked over to the sink where Mum was draining the veggies, but her mother waved her away.

'No, you stay and talk to your brothers. This is nothing. I'm used to serving up for a hundred at the pub.' Jenni looked back as Dane stood behind her and rested his chin on her shoulder and they watched Mum deftly drain, stir and season. It was a bit quieter away from the table, where Donny and Matt were in the midst of a heated discussion about finances.

'Already.' Mum rolled her eyes as she looked at her youngest and eldest sons as Matt put his beer bottle down heavily on the table.

'Oh, yum. Is that Karumba Pub peas, I can see?' Dane reached past Jenni and picked a cooked pea out of the saucepan.

Mum slapped his hand away. 'Yes, they are, but you can wait for your dinner, young man.' She laughed as she stared up at him. 'Just because you've grown so tall, doesn't mean you lose your manners.'

'And *bejesus* cauliflower too? Oh, Mum, I love you.' Dane reached over again and filched a baked potato out of the tray, and got his fingers slapped for that too.

'*Bejesus* cauliflower?' Jenni screwed her nose up. 'Is that something new on the pub menu?'

Mum shook her head with a laugh. 'No, but your brother has been eating at the pub a bit.' She winked at Jenni. 'Might have something to do with a certain waitress here, methinks.'

Dane shook his head. 'Nope, it's the fabulous food there. That's all.'

'So, tell me about these veggies,' Jenni asked with a laugh.

'Yeah, so you can cook them for us when Mum goes off on her travels.'

Jenni whacked him on the shoulder. 'I'm not cooking for anyone. Or if I do, we'll take it in turns.'

'Sugar, soda and salt in the peas, Jen,' Mum said. 'Makes them sweet and keeps them green.' She laughed again. 'And the short order cook before me said the only way to cook cauliflower was to cook the "bejesus" out of it, and your big brother loves it like that.'

'Soft and runny, yum.' Dane gave a satisfied sigh.

Jenni smiled as she looked around at her family. It was so good to be home. Life had been lonely in her apartment in Brisbane.

Mum pointed to the cutlery drawer. 'You can set the table now, Jen. 'It's almost ready.'

As Jenni turned to open the drawer, she froze as Mum called over to the table. 'Matthew, did you invite Jake?'

'I did, but he said he didn't want to impose.' Matt shot a glare at Dane, and Jenni felt him stiffen beside her.

'Good,' he muttered beneath his breath.

Mum turned around slowly. 'I heard that, Dane. And I'm disappointed in you. What sort of welcome is that for a man who's come back to town, and has no one here of his own?'

Dane shrugged but his voice was terse. 'So why did he come back?'

'That's his business and not ours.' Mum put the saucepan on the sink with a clatter. 'Matthew, you get over next door and tell Jake to get himself over here quick smart. I've cooked enough for him too. The poor boy's been over there by himself for a few days.'

As Matt nodded and headed out the door, Mum leaned back on the sink and folded her arms. 'And I expect the three of you to be polite and welcoming. I thought I brought my children up to be kind. And forgiving.'

Dane went to speak and obviously thought better of it. He reached out and raised his eyebrows at Jenni as he took the knives and forks from her hands.

Donny obviously felt he could put his opinion across. His voice was quiet and calm. 'I think to be fair, Mum, that Dane is thinking of Jenni's feelings.'

Their mother shook her head. 'Jenni's a big girl now. She doesn't need anyone speaking for her.' She raised her eyebrows. 'Do you, Jen?'

Jenni shrugged as Dane had. 'It's only dinner. I'm sure I'll survive one meal in Jake's company.'

'Just watch the silver,' Dane muttered as he crossed to set the table.

It was going to be an interesting meal.

She just had to survive it.

***

Jake argued, but Matt wouldn't listen. 'No, mate. I told you before, it's a family dinner.'

'You're invited.'

'I'm not tidy enough.'

'You'll do.'

'Just let me get changed then.' Jake headed across the deck, but Matt was close behind him.

Before he knew it, he was being dragged off the boat, in the direction of the McDougal house next door.

'I'm not going back without you. Mum will have my hide if I do.'

'Yeah, what about the rest of the family?' Jake could feel the tension building in his temples. He could deal with the fallout—it might be ten years later than he would have liked—but he worried about the impact on Jenni. They hadn't had a real conversation for ten years, let alone sat at a dinner table together.

In the house of his accuser.

'At least let me get changed, Matt.'

'Nah. You're fine as you are. Better than the corporate gear. Although I'd like to see Donny's face when he sees your boat.'

'Let me at least grab a six-pack.' Jake turned back to the boat.

'No, Mum's ready to serve up. Come on.'

'What did you say about Donny's face?' he asked as he trudged reluctantly behind Matt.

'He'll be green with envy. He wanted to upgrade the boats before Dad died, but Dad wouldn't have a bar of it. And then when he was gone, we could see why. The finances weren't there.'

'I'm impressed that you've kept the business going, between the four of you.'

'The three of us,' Matt replied. 'Jen has nothing to do with it. She won't even take her dividend from the family company each year, not that it's much. She insists that it goes back into the business.'

They reached the gate in the fence all too quickly. The McDougal house was out of sight from his place, around the bend in the river, away from Jake's home and jetty. So at least he hadn't had to see Jenni coming and going all week as he'd worked on *Moonshine*.

Matt obviously sensed his discomfort. 'It's okay, mate. We're all grownups now.'

Jake swallowed. 'Yeah. That we are.'

Matt pushed open the kitchen door and as Jake followed him in, the conversation came to an abrupt halt.

Sally McDougal walked over, untying her apron and put it on the duck cupboard next to the door. Jake smiled as he looked at the old cupboard that was supposed to hold shoes, but in the times that he had visited had had a plethora of what everybody dropped as they came in from outside.

He stood back looking at the collection of screwdrivers, keys, loose change and clothes pegs, and strangely he relaxed. Nothing had changed. As he looked across at Sally's big smile, the tension eased even more. Sally held her arms open and he folded her in a hug.

'You've grown up, Jakey.'

'I hope so, Sally.' Damn it, his voice was shaking and he could feel moisture building behind his eyes. He blinked it away before he embarrassed himself.

Jenni was standing by the fridge, a jar of sauce in each hand. He nodded at her; even if her mother expected him to hug Jenni, she'd made sure her hands were full. He knew her well.

Dane and Donny stood. He sensed the smiles were forced, but they each held out a hand in turn and shook his firmly.

'Sit down, everyone. It's all served up.' Sally gestured to the chair near the door. 'You sit there, Jake. Where you always did.'

The reference to the past killed the conversation again, and there was an awkward silence around the table as everyone took their seats. Thank goodness for Sally, who chatted as she carried the plates over to the table and placed a loaded dinner plate in front of each of them.

Finally, Donny spoke. 'Can I get you a drink, Jake? Beer? Soft drink? Water?'

He looked at what everyone else was drinking and nodded. 'A beer would be great, thank you.'

'So Jake, tell us all about your travels.' Sally's voice was bright as she gestured for them all to start eating.

Jake picked up his knife and fork. 'Not so much travels. I've been in the one spot for the last eight years. In the marina at Monte Carlo.'

'Half your luck.' Donny's voice held a note of curiosity. 'I've seen photos of some of the boats over there. Mega millions.'

Jake nodded as he sliced the succulent pork. It was a long time since he'd sat at a kitchen table and had a home-cooked meal. The first two years after he'd left Karumba had been spent in a variety of cheap boarding houses on the north Queensland coast as he'd completed his courses and worked on the boats. 'Yep, there's some money over there, that's for sure. If you ever wanted to travel, you'd have no trouble getting a job over there. They love the Aussies. We've got a reputation for having a work ethic.'

'Maybe one day.' Donny nodded.

Jake looked up surprised as Jenni spoke quietly. 'That's one place I'd like to go. France. Ever since we had Mrs MacLean in high school teaching us about French culture, I've wanted to go there. Paris in the spring is on my bucket list.' Her voice was dreamy. 'One day.'

Jake looked over at Sally as relaxation settled in his bones. The conversation was flowing around him, and there were lots of smiles. 'Thanks for the invite, Sally. It's a lovely meal.'

'So Matt tell us you're back to stay, Jake?' Dane's voice was careful.

Jake picked up his beer and took a sip before he answered. 'Yes, I'm home now.'

Okay, in for a penny, he thought. 'I've already mentioned it to Matt. I was going to come across and see you. To ask to meet with you all. I've got a business proposition you might be interested in.'

'Why would we want to go into business with you?' Dane was unsmiling. Jake looked up and caught Jenni looking at him intently. Warmth crept through him before she masked her expression and then dropped her gaze.

'The new legislation is going to open up Australian waterways to a lot of high-end competition. You're going to have to be able to offer something special if you want to keep the customers coming to you.'

Dane and Donny looked at each other before they turned to Matt. 'What legislation?'

Matt shrugged. 'I don't know. What are you referring to, Jake?

'I saw the headline on the ABC news online this morning. I knew nothing about it either, but it's going to have a huge impact on charters around the country.'

The three McDougal brothers frowned together, and Sally and Jenni exchanged a glance.

'What's happening, Jake?' Jenni's voice was soft.

He put his fork down and pulled out his phone. 'Excuse me for doing this at the dinner table, Sally, but it's pretty important.'

She nodded. 'Go ahead, Jake.'

He read aloud the news headline that had caught his attention that morning.

'International superyachts set to be attracted by possible tax break and 'virgin' cruising grounds.'

'Tax break?' Matt's frown increased. 'What sort of tax break?'

'Well, if I understand it properly—I've been away for a long time—under current laws, foreign-owned yachts that want to travel to Australia and operate charters have to pay the ten percent GST.'

Matt nodded. 'That's right. The way it stands now, anyone from overseas who wants to charter in

Australian waters has to pay the GST on the value of the boat.'

Dane chipped in. 'An owner sends his super yacht out and it might be worth a hundred million … so he's got to put ten million on the counter for the government before he can do anything.'

'That's the way it's always been, and it's made our fishing and cruising grounds not viable for international companies.'

Jake kept reading from the small screen in front of him. 'Charging the GST on a charter, instead of the yacht's value, would open up Australia to international vessels that traditionally operate in luxury hotspots such as the Mediterranean and Caribbean.'

Dane pushed his plate aside and picked up his beer. 'Holy hell. That's going to be huge for us. First I've heard of this. How the heck will we compete?'

'They say the legislation will be through in a couple of months.' Jake looked up and held Dane's eyes steadily. He was the brother who would need the most convincing. 'That's why I talked to Matt the other day. I've got a business suggestion that will position you uniquely up here.'

Dane's voice was full of suspicion. 'What would you want to help us out? Why don't you just want to take your cut of the business?'

'Two reasons.' Jake's throat was suddenly dry, and he picked up the carafe of water in the middle of the table. He filled his glass and drank before he answered, aware of five pairs of eyes on him.

'Because, it will also benefit my business, and—' he paused and looked at each of them —I owe this family.'

Jake was satisfied to see the flush that tinged Jenni's cheeks.

Chapter Eight

It was close to midnight when Jake finally left. Dane had thawed, and the conversation had been animated as they'd discussed the change in the charter boat legislation. Jenni had helped Mum clear the table and do the dishes and then helped serve up homemade apple crumble and custard. Jake had been polite, but distant, the couple of times she'd spoken to him. Now Jenni stood in the shadows by her bedroom window until he was out of sight. She wrapped her arms around herself not knowing how she felt.

Well, okay, she knew how she felt. She'd wanted to run after Jake, and have him hold her in his arms and kiss her like he'd used to. It was time to admit that to herself. Heck, he'd only been here seven days. Why had he really come back to the Bay? There was nothing here for him; his life in the Mediterranean must have been exciting. Way more exciting than a small backwater like Second Chance Bay would ever be.

International charter takeover or not.

She stared through the window and put her hand on the cool glass. The night was dark and the sky was brilliant with diamond stars. Memories overwhelmed her.

The first time Jake had kissed her, it had been on a clear winter night just like this one. Next to the gate he'd just closed behind him as he'd headed back to his flash boat.

It had been Mum's fortieth birthday, and the party had been in full swing. They'd managed to slip away from Dad's eagle eye. If Jenni had heard him say once that she was too young to have a boyfriend, she'd heard it a hundred times.

Besides he had nothing to worry about; she and Jake were only *friends*. Jake was a better friend to her than any of the girls at school; they loved the same things. She would walk along the river bank with him for hours chasing crabs—and avoiding crocodiles—and talking. Talking about his plans to build a life on the water, talking about her desire to study to be a teacher.

He treated her like one of the boys and his company was easy. Jake didn't know the thrill that went through her whenever he held her hand, or put his arm casually around her shoulders. To Jake, Jenni was a mate—simply another one of the McDougal boys.

Unable to settle, Jenni reached for a jacket and opened the sliding door that led from her bedroom to the verandah. She was too restless to sleep. The house was quiet; she could just hear the murmur of Mum's voice. She smiled; Mum had said she was going to make a phone call.

It was good to see her happy and making plans for the future. Mum had done it tough when Dad had been alive. Their life had been hard and rough; Mum deserved to have some happiness. She's been a fabulous mother to them, and everything she'd done had been for the four kids. Mum had sacrificed a lot for her family.

It was time she had time for herself. Even though Jenni had loved her father, she knew he had been a difficult man for Mum to live with. His boats had come first, his mates at the pub, his gambling, and then Mum and the kids came a sorry last. It had been sad for all of them when he'd died in his late fifties, but a life of hard drinking and hard living had caught up with him.

Her three brothers were good men. Growing up the way they had, had made them determined to live good lives. The only thing that Jenni worried about now was why they were all still living at home.

Each of them had had relationships, but like her, she suspected that they too had trust issues.

With a shrug, Jenni stepped out to the verandah and welcomed the fresh air.

The night was still and there was no moon, and it wasn't too cold so she left her jacket unzipped as she walked towards the water. Even though it was winter, she still kept an eye out for snakes. As she got closer to the McDougal jetty, she could see the lights of Jake's boat around the bend. His silhouette passed by one of the windows on the top deck as she stood watching, and a shaft of longing for the old easy days ran through her. When life was uncomplicated, and everyone got on. When there was no shadow from the past hanging over them. Jake stepped out onto the deck and held the railing staring in her direction. Even though it was dark and she knew he wouldn't be able to see her, Jenni stepped behind the clump of bushes at the side of the path.

Wide awake, she stared at the water; she knew that she was going to have trouble falling asleep tonight.

What had Jake meant when he said he owed the family?

Was it an admission of guilt? When he'd fled that had been enough of an admission for her. Her father might have been hard but he'd never lied to her.

Could she find it in herself to forgive Jake? Maybe he hadn't changed like she thought he had. Maybe circumstances had forced him to take the money from the shop.

Tears ached in Jenni's throat and she shook her head.

No.

No matter what had motivated Jake back then, she could never forgive him.

Dishonesty was a trait that she couldn't accept.

Even if she still cared about him. Even if he still made her heart sing.

He was not the man she'd thought he was. He never had been, and he never would be.

***

Jake couldn't sleep.

He was wired. Talking to the McDougals about the things they could do if they formed a partnership had been received so much better than he'd imagined in his wildest dreams. Even Dane had come around and shaken his hand as he'd left the McDougal home a couple of hours ago.

Jenni?

Jenni had been a different matter. Even at the end of the night, when they'd been relaxed, she'd been aloof. When he'd said goodbye, her eyes had been downcast and he knew that she didn't want him there.

She didn't want him in their home.

She didn't want him in Second Chance Bay.

She obviously didn't want him in her life.

Well, she was just going to have to get over it; he was here to stay.

He lay on the deck and looked up at the stars, cursing the man who had taken Jenni from him as he thought back.

##

February 2008

'Jake, come in.'

Jake stood outside the door of the office at McDougal's Fish Co-op. He knew the shop well; he'd been working there since he was sixteen. Mrs McDougal was behind the counter and she smiled at him absently as she bagged the fresh prawns that had just come in on the afternoon trawler.

'I'll give you a hand with that after Mr M speaks to me.'

Her smile had been distracted and sad. She'd obviously known what was about to ensue.

Jake had walked into the office and respectfully taken his cap off. As he held it by his side he glanced down at it— a navy blue cap with the McDougal logon on the front. He'd been lucky that the McDougals had taken him under their wing when he'd made friends with Donny at school.

'Sit down.' There was no welcome in Mr M's voice.

Jake frowned as he sat down. Maybe Mr M wasn't happy that he was heading off to college for a few weeks for some intensive training for his coxswain's certificate. He'd offered to make up the hours in the shop by doubling up before he went, and when he came back so that the boys were free to deckie on the family charter boats. Maybe he was embarrassed because he'd overheard some of the conversation with that sleazy guy who'd come in demanding to see Bob yesterday afternoon. Jake had ended up going outside when the conversation from the office had been heated. Luckily there were no customers in the shop. The guy was carrying on about paying debts as Jake had pushed the door open and gone outside for a while to give them some privacy.

The guy had stared at Jake and given him a mouthful as he'd left a few minutes later.

'What are you staring at, boy? You make sure your old man pays his debts or there'll be trouble.'

Jake had shrugged and gone back into the shop. He served for the next hour and then balanced the till before he left the cash in the bank bag in the drawer under the counter for Bob to collect on his way out.

He sat there and Bob McDougal stared at him over the desk, tapping a pen on the wooden top. Finally, he reached into the drawer and pulled out his chequebook.

'I'm not going to beat around the bush,' he said.

'In what way, sir?' Jake's mother might have been poor, and a single mother, but she'd taught her son respect and good manners.

'You've been seeing our Jenni.'

'Seeing?' Suddenly he swallowed; he intended to marry Jenni McDougal when he had enough money, and when he had his own business behind him. But not before then.

'My wife saw you.'

'Saw me?'

'Last month at her birthday party.' McDougal glared at him and Jake lifted his chin. They were nineteen years old and he'd done nothing wrong.

'You were kissing my daughter at the gate between our two properties when you snuck out of the party.'

It was the first time that Jake had kissed Jenni, and it had been a special moment, and he didn't appreciate it being sullied by being spied on, and by being accused of sneaking around.

He wasn't a kid to be chastised. He lifted his chin and held her father's gaze steadily.

'Yes. I kissed your daughter. But as we are both adults, so I don't see a problem with that.'

'I took you on because I thought you could do with some pocket money. It wasn't an invitation to infiltrate yourself into my family. My daughter is not going end up with river trash.' McDougal's voice was as cold as the ice in the cabinets in the room beside them.

Jake stood, pushing the chair back as hot fury flooded his veins. 'I beg your pardon?'

'You heard me, boy. River trash. The Jones always have been and always will be. You will not taint my daughter with a connection to your family.'

Jake stood there unable to believe what he was hearing. He opened his mouth but McDougal yelled at him before he could speak.

'Sit down and listen.' The words were spat at him.

McDougal opened the cheque book and wrote quickly. Jake stayed standing, the only noise in the room apart from the blood surging through his temples was the scratching of the pen on the paper. McDougal stood, ripped the cheque from the cheque book, and shoved it at Jake.

'Take this, and leave town. I don't want to see you around here—or around any of my kids again.'

Jake stared down at the cheque that was now in his hands unable to believe what he'd just heard. The bell on the shop door tinkled as he stood there.

Two thousand dollars.

'Take it and get out. And don't mention it to anyone or you'll be sorry. Go and do your course, and get a job in a different town. Second Chance Bay is not for you.'

Jake had slowly lifted the cheque as McDougal stared at him, his face red, and the smell of alcohol wafting on his breath across the desk. He'd held the man's gaze as he'd torn it into small pieces. Holding his hand above the desk Jake let the scraps of paper flutter down to the desk.

'Don't you ever speak to me like that again, and don't you ever try to buy me out. I won't be working here again until you apologise for the way you spoke about my family.'

Even if he'd known what was going to happen, he wouldn't have reacted in any other way.

Jake had pushed the chair out of his way, turned on his heel and shoved the door open.

He ignored the customers in the shop and the offer of bagging prawns was long forgotten as he ran for the dock, and jumped into his small aluminium tinnie.

He crossed the river to go home to their old house at Second Chance Bay to lick his wounds.

River trash.

Old man McDougal would pay for that.

Chapter Nine

Jenni pushed open the door of the fish co-op and the bell jangled above the door. Matt had gone back to Normanton to see the accountant, but this time Maisie from the caravan park had been available to take over for the day. Jenni was here to relieve her for a lunch break because Mum was busy packing. Now that everyone was home, she and Rick had decided to set off sooner. Rick had turned up the other night towing a brand-new off-road caravan that had been delivered from Brisbane on the back of a huge truck.

'He's obviously got a quid. Owns a few pubs in the north,' Matt said to Jenni as Rick led Mum to the van, his hands over her eyes. A lump filled Jenni's throat as she watched Mum giggle like a teenager.

'She's so happy. It wouldn't matter if he was broke,' she said with a smile.

'True, but Mum's had enough years of that,' Matt said. 'It's time she got a bit spoiled.'

They followed the couple to the van and smiled as their mother exclaimed over the luxury interior.

'Oh my God, look, there's even a washing machine,' she cried as they poked their heads around the door. Rick had smiled as Mum looked around inside, and then he beckoned to Jenni and Matt. He stepped along the footpath away from the van.

'I want to head off earlier than we'd planned. I know you've just got home, Jenni. Will it work okay with you guys if we leave next week?'

Jenni nodded. 'Of course, it will. We're all grownups now.' She put her hand on Rick's arm and reached up to brush his cheek with a light kiss. 'Thank you, Rick. Mum is so happy.'

'I'm a very lucky man. Sally is a good woman.' He lowered his voice. 'And I plan to make an honest woman of her, so who do I ask for permission in the family?'

'Permission for what?' Matt said blankly.

'For permission to marry her, of course!'

Happiness ran through Jenni and she hugged Rick.

'Don't say anything; I'm going to surprise her tonight.' Rick's grin was wide.

'Well, of course, you have permission. I'm the eldest and I say yes.' Matt shook Rick's hand. 'Absolutely yes! I'm very happy for you both too.'

Rick had done the deed, and of course, Mum accepted and was now sporting a massive engagement ring, and busily packing the caravan.

Jenni sighed as she crossed to the counter. Mum was just bubbling with happiness.

'Hi Maisie.'

'Young Jenni! I heard you were home.' Maisie's hair was silver and purple as it had always been, but the lines in her face were a little deeper.

'Not so young anymore.' Jenni walked around and hugged the elderly woman who had befriended the family before Jenni was born. It was over thirty years since she and her husband had first made the trek from Melbourne to Karumba for their annual winter holiday.

Jenni took a deep breath of fresh air as she walked behind the counter. The ever-present smell of nicotine, and Avon perfume was as strong as ever.

'I've missed you, love. Are you home for a visit? Or home to stay?'

'I'm not sure yet.' Jenni changed the subject before she had to answer more questions. 'I hear you've finally moved sites.'

She was answered with a cackle that quickly turned into a smoker's cough. When Maisie recovered, her grin was wide. 'Yeah, love, since my Jack passed away my fun days are over. You heard right though. I've moved the van down to Dunrootin' Lane the past couple of winters.'

Jenni shook her head with a wide grin. 'It's been called that so long they need a street sign up.'

'Nah, a lot of the old codgers find it offensive, they don't know how to have a good laugh at themselves. Now, I'll go and have myself some lunch and a smoke over at the pub. What time do you want me back?'

Jenni shook her head. 'Don't worry about it. I've got nothing else to do. I'll take over for the afternoon if you like.'

'Ooh, you're a good girl. I'll go and play the pokies for a while. If I have a win I'll split it with you.'

'No need.'

Maisie refused to take any money when she filled in at the shop. She always said that it was her daily entertainment talking to the grey nomies as they rolled into town, and always bought fresh prawns on their first day in Karumba. She slipped the plastic apron off and passed it over to Jenni. 'They tell me that nice young man of yours has come back to town too. Is that why you came back?'

Jenni forced out a laughing response. 'Jake Jones? Oh heavens, no. I didn't even know he'd come back. I haven't seen him since I left.'

'I hear he left his fancy boat in France to come back and work with your brothers.

Jenni played dumb and widened her eyes. Honestly, this town had a grapevine like nothing she'd ever seen anywhere else. 'I think Jake's boats are too flash for us.'

Maisie tapped her nose. 'Wouldn't hurt you blokes to have a flash boat.'

'It's up to the boys what they do.' Jenni shrugged. 'I'm here to teach.' She looked at the display cabinet with a grin. 'And to serve prawns when my brother heads out of town.'

'If Matt ever decides to go on the boats, you might find yourself in here full time. It'd be better than being in a classroom with a heap of kids all day.

Anything would be better than that in my books.' Maisie's cackle filled the air as the door shut behind her, the smell of Avon perfume lingering.

'There's no chance of that ever happening,' Jenni muttered.

The bell over the door tinkled again and she looked up hoping it might be Matt home early.

Her breath caught in her chest as her gaze encountered the sexy hazel eyes of Jake Jones.

***

'Hi Jenni.' Jake closed the door behind him. 'I was hoping to see Matt.'

She shook her head. 'I'm sorry. You're out of luck. He's gone to Normanton for an appointment.

'Damn. I've got a problem I was hoping he could help me with.'

'Oh?' Jenni was looking past him at the door as though she was hoping he would use it. Her voice was cold and disinterested, and Jake's temper began to simmer.

Who did she think she was to treat him as though he was the river trash that her father had called him ten years ago?

Jenni wasn't the same person she'd been back then. Jake bit down on the cross words that threatened and crossed to the counter. He stood there quietly looking at her until Jenni finally looked at him.

'So, what's the problem?' she said.

'My other boat is on the way down the Gulf, and I'm down a crew member. I was hoping that I could borrow one of your hostesses for my first charter in a few days. I know the boys haven't got another charter for a couple of weeks.

Finally, the bland look left her face as one eyebrow quirked, but her mouth was still set in a tight line. 'You know more about what's happening with our bookings than I do.'

'I wouldn't say that,' he said. 'And I didn't know I'd be down a crew member till Gus rang me just now.'

'Gus?'

'My other captain. And a good mate of mine too.' Jake leaned against the counter. 'I interviewed in Darwin before we headed over here and I was all set, but one of my hostesses broke her arm yesterday. The seas were rough on the way across from Bathurst Island, and she slipped on the wet deck.' Jake ran a hand over his short-clipped hair. 'I want this first charter to be perfect, Jen. It's important to me.'

She nodded and her voice thawed a little. 'I'm sure it is.'

'So, I'm after a hostess. Do you know who works for them? Anyone local or do they fly in?

'A hostess?' Jenni smiled at last. 'What does a hostess do?'

'Serves the meals, clears the tables, services the cabins. Oh, and does the guests' laundry. And works behind the bar and tallies up the drinks every night.'

'Hm, really? I think you might be used to a different level of service in your European marinas.'

This time it was a chuckle that bubbled out and Jake relaxed a bit more.

'Dane and Donny and the deckies do all that,' Jenni said. 'And the guests wash their own clothes. At least we offer a washing machine and dryer on the boats. Our charters are rough and ready. For the true fishermen, not for someone looking for a fancy five star holiday.'

'So they're not going to be able to suggest anyone by the sound of things. Damn.' Disappointment ran through Jake. 'Maybe I could find someone in town? Backpackers?'

Jenni shook her head. 'The town's changed Jake. All old locals and grey nomies now. We don't get many backpackers up this way. It's too far off the beaten track and there's not a lot of entertainment at night. Even the Animal Bar is a quiet place for a drink these days. The attraction of the wild and unruly in that famous song has long gone.'

'I'd forgotten about that Red Hot Chili Peppers' song. We thought back then it'd put our town on the international map. Do they still bolt the furniture down in case of bar fights?

Jenni shook her head. 'No. I think if you go there now, according to Maisie you might find a few old locals having a quiet beer or playing the pokies. The town has really changed, Jake. Are you sure you want to start your business here?'

'I'm home, Jenni,' he said simply. 'This is my dream. This is why I've worked so hard over the past ten years.' He looked at her curiously; she obviously wasn't happy about him being home and he wanted to reassure her. 'I'm not going to be competition to your family's business. I want to add to it and I want to help out.'

'So you say.' Her shoulders were straight and her demeanour was still stiff, despite the occasional smile and chuckle.

'Well, you're going to struggle. Matt can't even get a casual to work in the shop. There's only Maisie.'

'And you.' His voice was glum. An idea began to flit though his head as he stared at Jenni. 'When do you start at the school?"

Her eyes narrowed. 'Who told you I was working at the school?'

'Matt, I think it was. Your brothers are all proud of you getting an education, and being a teacher.' Jake pushed himself away from the counter. 'So am I.'

Jenni didn't answer but he noticed the flush tinge her cheeks pink. She wasn't as aloof as she was making out.

'So when do you start?'

She shrugged. 'When school goes back in three weeks. I'll only be working at the local school for a little while. And then I'll go back to Brisbane. That's my home now.' She lifted her chin and her gaze was steady.

A burst of warmth fired in Jake's chest, and moved down to his belly as her blue eyes held his for a long moment.

'So you're at a loose end for the next couple of weeks?' he said. 'How would you like to come out on *Moonshine* for a five day charter? Help me out, and we could spend some time getting to know each other again.'

Jenni didn't answer for a moment, but Jake held his breath as the tip of her tongue came out and she moistened her top lip.

'Not really. Do you really think I'd work on *your* boat?'

The warmth inside him changed instantly from desire to anger.

'Why, Jenni? Aren't I good enough for you?' His voice was curt as hurt slammed through him

'I didn't mean that.'

'Didn't you? Sure sounded like it to me. Echoes of the past, hey?' He turned on his heel and called over his shoulder as he pushed the door open. 'Get Matt to call me, if it's not too much trouble in your busy schedule.'

Chapter Ten

The door closed quietly behind Jake and Jenni's hair fell over her face as she lowered her head. She gripped the counter so hard her knuckles whitened, and guilt ran through her. She had been overly rude, and she knew that she'd hurt Jake's feelings. He'd never had that attitude of not being good enough before he'd left. Maybe coming back to town had made him realise he'd done the wrong thing.

Not only by the McDougals but also by the values that she thought he held.

Jake Jones had to have a reason for coming back to town, and she didn't trust him. All this talk of working with her brothers and helping out the family business made no sense.

Why would someone who was obviously as successful as he was want to come back to Second Chance Bay and work with the very people he'd done the wrong thing by?

There was something not right about the whole thing, but there was no way Jenni was going to sit back and let Jake hurt her family again.

And for all his soft looks, and his "I'm proud of you," she wasn't going to let him get close enough to hurt her again.

No way.

Jake Jones could remain at a distance, but by God, she was going to find out why he was here.

The shop was empty so she grabbed a bottle of water from the drinks cabinet and headed out the back.

A stupid move. As she lowered the water bottle, she stared down at the dock. After Mum's party, the afternoons Jake had been in the shop, and Dad had been safely out in the Gulf fishing, Jake would ring up the till and close up. Jenni would wait and they'd sit on the dock together and watch the sunset. No matter how long you lived at Karumba, the stunning sunsets were different each day. There was always a group of tourists at the pub on the point watching the fishing boats come home and enjoying the sea breeze under the lovely cool shade of the coastal almond trees. Jake and Jenni had spent so many afternoons of that last year before life had changed, sitting on the dock waiting for the sun to set in a spectacular golden ball over the silver waters of the Gulf.

She couldn't help smiling as she remembered Jake would count down as it got lower and lower, and the instant the sun slipped behind the horizon, he would hold her close and kiss her.

But only if Dad's boat was out of sight. It was crazy, but Jenni knew deep down that Dad wouldn't approve of them being in love.

Because she was in love with Jake Jones and in that last year, they had planned a future together.

Young love and foolish dreams. That's all it had been. She had been naïve and vulnerable. The only thing she was grateful for was that she'd never slept with him.

Coming home had raised so many different memories. Things that she could put aside when she was in Brisbane, but being back here, there was a happy memory everywhere she turned.

If she could discover why Jake was really here, maybe she'd be able to move on. Maybe she could finally get over him, and be happy.

Ten years was way too long to mourn over a lost relationship. Jenni knew it had made her bitter, and the way she'd argued with her brothers since she'd arrived home was a sign that she needed to lift herself.

She was turning into a shrew.

"My tongue will tell the anger of my heart, or else my heart concealing it will break." When she'd taught *'Taming of the Shrew'* to her English class last term, she knew that described her so well. She had to learn to temper her words. Her broken heart was long ago and in the past.

From now on she'd make an effort to be pleasant.

To everyone.

##

'Two more days, and we'll be on the road.' Sally wiped a hand over her weary face as Jenni walked into the kitchen. 'I'll be glad to take a break.'

Jenni looked around the kitchen and then back at her mother. Casserole dishes covered the benchtops and a huge pot of something delicious was bubbling on the stove. The oven was glowing red, and the smell of cakes baking mingled with the stew.

'What are you doing? You do know you can cook in the caravan?' Jenni walked over and kissed her mother's cheek before she peeked in the pot on the stove. 'You told me it had an oven too, didn't you?'

Sally waved her hand before she turned back to the sink. 'No, this is for all of you. You'll be busy when you start at school, and you've probably forgotten the boys' favourite meals. Dane likes curry, Donny prefers chilli and Matt—'

'Whoa. Stop right there.' Jenni put her hands on her hips and stared at her mother with disbelief, but Mum kept talking.

'And Matt has a sensitive stomach, so just plain casserole for him. He always has had, but you probably didn't know that. And when you iron their jeans, Matt doesn't like creases in his, but the other two do.'

The front door opened and Jenni waited until the footsteps came down the hall. Matt poked his head around the doorway and smiled.

'How was the shop this afternoon, Jen? Busy?'

He walked into the kitchen, followed closely by Dane and Donny. Matt opened the fridge and pulled out three beers.

She stared at her three brothers and her eyes narrowed. Before she could answer they all sat down at the kitchen table and popped open the tops of their stubbies. Her hands clenched as she walked across and stood behind Matt's chair.

'So how should I know that? Didn't you think Maisie was going to be in the shop all day?'

Matt raised his beer. 'I knew you'd stay there after she went for lunch and then I saw her old Datsun at the pub in town.'

Remember, I am not going to be a shrew.

Jenni's voice was very controlled as she regarded her eldest brother. 'So you know me well, do you, Matt? And what about you pair? Do you know how rude you are?' She looked at Donny, who had the grace to look a bit ashamed. Dane was looking down at his beer. 'Maybe Mum who's been slaving over a hot stove all day, so you can eat while she is a thousand kilometres away, would have liked a drink too? Maybe I'd like a beer. You should be over in the animal bar at the pub, you've got no manners!'

Matt stood and clomped to the fridge. 'Would you like a drink, Mum? Sorry.'

'No, I'm fine, thank you.' Mum frowned at her. 'Jenni, what's got up your nose? You've been cranky ever since you came home. Are you feeling well, love?'

A ripple of guilt ran through Jenni. Yes, she had been seemed cranky ever since she'd come home. Bickering with her brothers, and being oversensitive. The not-be-a-shrew affirmation hadn't lasted long.

'I'm sorry,' Jenni said quietly as she took the beer that Matt held out, and pulled out a chair. 'You sit down, Mum. I'll wash the dishes while you have a break.'

'We'll do it together.' Mum stood behind her chair.

Dane looked at Donny, and then they both looked at Matt. 'We'll do the dishes while you both sit down,' he said

By the look on Mum's face, it was the first time that had happened for a long while.

'Thank you,' she said slowly. 'And okay, I will have a wine.' She turned to Jenni. 'Now madam, tell me why you're so upset with your brothers.' Mum hadn't called her madam for years, and the guilt settled more heavily in Jenni's chest. Maybe she should have stayed in Brisbane and looked for a job in another rural area. But the thought of coming home had seen her through a couple of difficult terms at the inner-city school where she'd been a contract casual teacher.

'I'm sorry. You all wore my temper. I'll keep it in check from now on.' Jenni held up a warning finger. 'But that still doesn't mean I'll be cooking and washing up and ironing your jeans for you when Mum goes.'

'We don't expect you to,' Dane said. 'We are quite capable.'

Jenni made a sound a cross between a snort and a laugh. 'I'm pleased to hear that. Besides I won't be here for a week after Mum leaves.'

'Where are you going?' Mum looked worried. 'You haven't changed your mind about working at the school, have you?'

Jenni shook her head. 'No. I'm going out on Jake's first charter as a hostess.' There was no need to tell them she'd just decided that.

Mum choked on her wine, and a flurry of suds landed on Matt's face as he dropped the pan he was scrubbing.

'What?' Dane's voice was quiet. 'Why would you do that?'

'Because I'm the only one in this family who seems to be concerned about what Jake Jones is up to. Why is he so fired up to work with you three? I don't believe a word he says when he reckons he's here because he owes us. So I'm going to see what he's up to.'

Chapter Eleven

Dane had looked thoughtful when Jenni had asked about Jake's motives, but Matt and Donny had sprung to Jake's defence.

'For goodness' sake, Jen. What's your problem?' Matt shook his head. 'Give the bloke a chance, he's been bloody generous with what he's offered us since he hit town.'

Jenni shook her head. 'No one does things like without a good reason.' She jumped as Mum put her wine glass down with a thud.

'I'm going to bed. I'm tired. Your dinner is on the stove.' She looked at Jenni. 'Would you please put the leftovers in the casserole dishes and put them in the freezer.'

Jenni and the boys were quiet as Mum put her glass in the sink and left the kitchen without a backward glance.

'Now look what you've—'

'Matt. Button it.' Dane's voice was low and firm. 'Everyone just pull back and be a bit thoughtful.'

Matt ran a hand through his tousled curls. He was the only one of the four who had inherited Mum's thick dark curls and her soft nature. 'I'm sorry. I think we're all tired and a bit stressed. But I just want to say one thing.' He turned to Jenni. 'If you insist on going out on Jake's boat, you think long and hard about why you're doing it. If you have an ulterior motive, it's not the right thing to do.'

'I'll be helping out,' she said quietly. 'He came to see you today because his hostess has a broken arm. He actually *asked* me to do it.'

Matt raised his eyebrows. 'I suppose that's okay then.'

After dinner was over and the kitchen cleaned up, her brothers headed to the lounge to watch the news. Mum's door was closed and Jenni stood outside for a moment, tempted to knock but there was no sound coming from inside.

She needed to tell Jake she was going to accept his offer before he changed his mind or found someone else. If her brothers were going to be so trusting, it was up to her to make sure that they were not going to find themselves in something they weren't prepared for.

Jenni closed the front door quietly behind her and headed across the yard. The gate opened with a creak and she paused as she looked at the jungle of long grass on the other side of the fence. As she stood there wishing she'd brought a pair of boots she spotted a flattened path where Jake had made his way over to their place. Slipping through the gate, she glanced across to the old Jones' house. Eerie shadows darkened the verandah on this side, and as she paused there was a scurry of movement in the long grass near the door. Jenni put her head down and followed the flattened grass towards the water, trying not to think of the creatures that could be around.

The boat was in darkness and she wondered if Jake was out. But as she stood there, a light flicked on the upper deck, so she swallowed and walked the last fifty metres to the jetty.

She shook her head. The jetty didn't look safe. The posts were rotten, and it sagged lower on one side.

Why on earth had Jake moored the luxury boat here?

The river was dark and shadowy, and as she approached the jetty, there was a swirl in the water just to her left. She jumped and picked up the pace. When she'd been a kid she'd seen crocodiles climb the high bank and bask in the sunshine on the grass flats above the river; surely they'd not be up here at night?

Not willing to take the risk, she put her head down and ran the last few metres to the timber jetty.

'Jake?' Her breath caught as a bright beam of light was directed her way. 'Are you there?' she called out.

'Jenni?' Jake stepped off the boat onto the dock and walked towards her. 'What's up? Everything okay?'

She nodded, suddenly feeling awkward. 'Yes, I just wanted to talk to you about what you said this afternoon.'

'Yes?' His voice was wary.

'I've decided to help you out. If you still want me to. With the hostess position, that is. I mentioned it to Matt and he said'—Jenni crossed her fingers behind her back— 'that he didn't know anyone.' She had mentioned it to Matt, and that's what he would have said if they hadn't descended into an argument, but she still felt guilty bending the truth. She wasn't being entirely honest, but Jake certainly didn't need to know her reasons.

*****

Jake was trying to act low-key. When he'd spotted Jenni coming towards the boat, his heart had sped up. He tried to talk sense to himself and remember the reception he'd had from her since he'd arrived.

'Yeah, sure. Let's talk. But not out here. Come aboard.' He held out his hand. 'Take my hand. Watch where you step; a lot of the planks are rotten. I'd hate to see you end up in the water. I need to get some light rigged up here before the others arrive tomorrow.'

He ignored the twitch as the nerves in his arm jumped when Jenni's cold fingers took his. He led her along the wharf to the far end where Moonshine's stern was protected from hitting the jetty by an inflatable barrier. 'I actually just saw a big croc surface close to the boat.'

'I heard it.'

She let go of his hand as soon as she stepped aboard. Knowing the rules of a boat, she bent down and slipped her thongs off.

'Let me put some lights on and then we'll go and sit inside. It's a bit cool out here on the water tonight.' He looked back at her as she followed him quietly. 'I'm pleased you came over, Jen.'

She nodded as he flicked on the bank of lights that lit the saloon and the middle deck. Jenni's indrawn breath was satisfying. Her eyes were wide and round as she looked around, and Jake was grateful that he had taken such care in choosing the interior for the boat. His gaze followed hers and he saw his boat through fresh eyes. The cream-colored drapes that covered the large windows facing the side decks were open so he crossed the room and pressed the switch and they slid closed quietly. Plush burgundy leather sofas that would seat a crowd of eighteen people comfortably formed two squares around the two circular glass coffee tables. On the front wall was a long timber bench where Jake had been working on his laptop when he'd heard her approaching. Fully expecting Matt, he'd been taken aback to see Jenni approaching the jetty.

The windows facing the bow were set high in the wall and curved around to follow the semi-circular shape of the front deck. Moonlight poured in and reflected on the crystal lamp on the bench beneath the window. Jake crossed over and gathered his papers together and put them in a folder, and closed the computer as Jenni watched quietly.

'I was just working on a logo for the bookings website,' he said. 'My web designer has suggested "Exotic Fishing in the Tropics" for a tagline. What do you think?'

Jenni shrugged but he noticed interest flare in her eyes before she looked away. 'Sounds fine to me.'

'Would you like to have a look around the boat before we talk? You can decide then if it suits you.'

Jake couldn't believe that Jenni had come over to say she would help him out. If she was serious, he'd play it cool, but inside he was turning somersaults at her offer. One, because he really needed someone, but second, the thought of having Jenni on the boat with him for five days—even though there would be others around—would give him an opportunity to show her that he was still the guy she'd always known.

It would be hard; there was no way he would ever tell her or any of the McDougal family that Bob had set him up. The man was dead and gone, and it wouldn't be fair to the family to taint their memories of him. There would be nothing to be gained by it. But by his behaviour, and his hard-earned success, Jake knew he could show Jenni that he was a decent, honest and trustworthy man.

At least that's what he hoped for.

Maybe there was a chance that they could revive the feelings that they'd once had for each other, because he'd known the minute that he'd seen her—

closed face, cold reception and all—that she was still the person that he had loved. They might have been young, but the feelings that he'd had for Jenni had been strong. Jake had never experienced it again, no matter how hard he'd searched for love in the last ten years.

One look at Jenni, and he'd known she was still in his heart—where she'd always been.

'Yes, I would.' She nodded and looked around and her voice thawed. 'This is really lovely, Jake.'

Hearing her say his name in that slightly husky voice warmed his heart.

He held out his hand, and was surprised when she took it again. 'Come on then, I'll give you the grand tour. And then can I offer you dinner? I was about to stop and eat. Or have you eaten?'

One side of her lips lifted in a quirky smile. 'Sort of.'

'Sort of?' Jake tried not to stare too hard at her face. She was still beautiful; her eyes were bright, and her dark lashes lowered as she shook her head. Her high cheekbones held a tinge of pink, and he wasn't sure if it was the sun, or being with him that had caused the slight flush. He could only hope.

'Don't ask. I was busy fighting with the boys. Poor Mum got upset, and went to bed, so I didn't feel like eating.'

Jake laughed. 'You lot never change. I thought your Mum would be used to your bickering by now. I got so used to you all fighting when we were kids, I could ignore it.'

'But that's the point. We're grown up now. We should be more mature and be able to get on without arguing all the time. Although—her lips quirked again—'the boys were in the wrong and I gave them a serve about making so much work for Mum.'

'It's families, Jen. It means you care about each other.'

'Maybe. It's just that we never agree. On anything.'

Jake's voice was quiet. 'Enjoy it. I was always envious of you being part of a large family when I was a kid. I guess I tried too hard to be a part of it.' He didn't want to say too much, but this was an opportunity not to be passed up. He could start letting Jenni know the truth without telling her the details. 'But no matter what happened, I'll always be grateful to your family for the start I got in life.'

Things were getting too serious, so he shook his head and smiled down at her.

He tugged on her hand. 'Follow me.

Showing off the rest of *Moonshine* was satisfying. After seeing the guest accommodation, the staff cabins, the stainless-steel commercial galley, and the wide fishing deck, Jenni even asked to see the engine room. Everything he showed her was new and sleek and spotlessly clean.

'And a lazerette storage area too! She's beautiful, Jake. You've done very well for yourself. Is the other boat the same?'

'A little bit smaller. This is the one I'll live on until I get the house done.'

'The house?'

He gestured to the shore. 'Mum's house. I'm going to do it up and live there. That way if the two boats are out on charters, when I hire more skippers, I'll have a home base.'

'Oh. So you are serious about settling back in the Bay?'

'I am.' He grinned and tried to lighten the heavy atmosphere that seemed to keep coming back. 'Now while we talk about the hostess job, let me feed you.'

She held up her hand and shook her head. 'No. I'm fine. Just give me the details. That is, if you still need me.'

Jake nodded. 'Oh, I do. And I'm grateful for your offer. I accept.' He stared at her and this time she held his gaze. 'But I must admit I'm surprised, Jen. I thought you weren't too interested when I mentioned it this afternoon.'

Her glance flicked away from his, the tip of her tongue appeared and his interest quickened. He knew her so well still; she was lying to him about something.

'Oh, I thought I'd help out. It'll be nice to be out on the water again. And the main thing that decided me is that Mum will be gone and the boys will have to fend for themselves.' Her smile was forced. 'And this is certainly a better option that the poor old tired *Sally M.* Have the boys seen the boat yet?'

'Not really, Matt had a quick squiz before I came over for dinner. Dane and Donny are coming over tomorrow.'

Her eyebrows rose but she didn't say anything.

'Now before we talk, I'm going to get my dinner. I'm starving.'

'Okay. That's fine.' Jenni looked at Jake with a frown as he crossed to the door that led out to the lower deck.

'Come with me. It's still in the water.'

Jenni held her breath as Jake leaned over the bow; if he leaned any further he'd go head first into the dark water. Her fingers itched to go over and hold his hips to keep him balanced like she would have done once. The tide was roaring in and the water was swirling around the boat, and it moved a little on the mooring. She stared as he straightened up. He pulled in the crab pot, and his biceps bulged and she couldn't help lowering her gaze to the strong thighs encased in snug fitting jeans.

Jenni's mouth dried and she fought licking her lips again as he turned to her, a triumphant grin lighting up his face. She was going to have to put a stop to these physical reactions if she was going to be spending five days—and nights— in his company.

'Two beauties! Look at these, Jen.'

She crossed the deck and leaned on the rail beside him. Two huge mud crabs were clicking and moving in the trap he'd pulled in. Their dark shells glistened green and dark blue in the moonlight as they snapped and tried to escape. Their walking legs, covered with lightly patterned dots, were getting caught in the mesh of the trap as Jake held them up.

'They're huge! I'd forgotten how big crabs get up here.'

'These are the biggest I've caught yet.' His grin was cheeky and a ripple of warmth ran down Jenni's spine as he held her eyes with his. 'I haven't been able to help myself. I've had crab for dinner every night—apart from your Mum's baked tea— since I arrived. The seafood in Europe is very different to here.'

'Is it? I hope you're not too hungry because they're going to take a while to cook and cool down before they'll be ready to eat,' she replied.

Jake's teeth flashed in the moonlight, and she couldn't help thinking what a good-looking man he'd become.

'This is the third lot of booty for the night. The others are cooked and cooling down in the fridge. I was going to drop in some crabs for your mum. I remembered how much she loved them when your brothers and I used to go crabbing. Her chilli crab was to die for.'

'And me,' Jenni said softly. 'I used to come with you too.'

'Did you come with us? I don't remember.' Jake's face screwed up in a frown as he tipped the crabs into a large bucket.

That was like a dash of cold water, and the happy warmth that had begun to envelop Jenni disappeared. She watched as Jake cleaned the deck down with the towel again. No wonder the place looked so good; Jake had cleaned up every drop of water that had splashed from the trap and the bucket. It was a wonder he was going to take them into the galley and cook on that pristine surface. She couldn't help compare it with the McDougal boats. The metal rivets on their decks had rusted from years in the salt water, and the decks were stained with the evidence of the many fish caught during hundreds of charters. Dad hadn't been too particular about the upkeep of the boats as long as there was beer on board, fish to be caught and paying customers.

'I also bought a feed of Gulf banana prawns off the trawler this afternoon. Can I tempt you? I won't feel right eating in front of you.'

Jenni smiled ruefully. 'And I suppose you went to the trawler because the witch in the fish shop was so cranky.

He shook his head with a laugh as he stowed the crab trap in a hatch, and then reached for a large towel to wipe off the side of the boat. 'Okay, she might have been a bit unfriendly, but I wanted to go and catch up with the guys on the trawlers too. '

'I'm sorry.' Jenni kept her voice quiet. From now on, she'd make a supreme effort to be pleasant.

Get thee behind me, shrew!

She'd be the smiling hostess, no matter how hard it was. If Jake trusted her, she could get to the bottom of why he was home.

'That's okay, Jen. It's been a long time.'

Chapter Twelve

If anyone had told Jenni that she'd be sitting on a luxury cruiser beneath a full moon with Jake Jones eating huge Gulf prawns a week after she arrived home from Brisbane, she would have said they were crazy.

But here she was, sitting at a polished timber table, eating off fine gold-rimmed white china, as prawn juice ran down her fingers. She nodded her thanks as Jake picked up a linen serviette and passed it to her. As she wiped her hands he stood and cleared the dishes away.

'So tell me more about the trip. Where's the charter going? How many guests, and what sort of clothes do you want the hostesses to wear?' she asked.

Jake rinsed his hands at the sink and came back over and sat down across from her. 'Before we talk business do you want to go and have a wash?' Jenni nodded and stood, trying to remember where the closest bathroom was.

'Use the powder room off the deck. It's the closest.'

'Thank you.' Jenni went out onto the deck, looking for the door Jake had pointed out when he had given her the tour. A cool breeze had sprung up and the temperature had dropped a few degrees, and she pulled her light cardigan round her shoulders.

Pushing open the door, her eyes widened and she shook her head as she entered the spacious powder room.

Gleaming white basins and fuchsia-pink guest towels lined the back wall. She bit back a grin, wondering if it would look like this after a few fish had been caught on deck and the guests came down here to clean up. At the same time, she marvelled at how well the boat was set up and how well it was kept. Jake was here alone this week, so he must keep it like this. He could teach the McDougal brothers a thing or two.

Soon it would be her job. For a moment she wondered if she was being foolish. How much would she be able to find out while Jake was busy with charter guests and she was working to keep the boat cleaned, and the guests happy? She straightened her shoulders as she washed her hands; she would do it.

A sweet fragrance drifted in the air, and her eyes opened further as she turned and spotted the fresh white Asian lilies in a glass vase on the table beside a pile of thick white towels. As Jenni looked back at the oval gilt-edged mirror, she started with surprise. Her cheeks were flushed and her eyes were bright. She looked . . . animated.

With a frown, she wiped her hands, before rinsing her face and patting it dry. She ran her hand over her hair, smoothing back the loose tendrils that had come out of her ponytail. She straightened the towel on the rail and headed back to the dining room.

It was time to get to business.

##

Jake insisted on walking Jenni back to the house after they had made the arrangements for the charter. It would leave in three days, when the guests arrived by light plane. It was the same day that Rick and Mum planned to head west.

'Call over and pick up your uniform when the other boat comes in tomorrow. And you can meet the other crew members too,' Jake said.

As they reached the gate, he put out a hand and touched her arm lightly. 'I really appreciate what you're doing, Jen. You've got me out of a fix.'

She cleared her throat and went to step back, but Jake circled her wrist gently with his fingers and tugged her closer.

'Not a problem. You want to help us, I can repay the favour,' she said and tried to smile. Her heart was thudding as his fingers slid down and held her hand.

He shook his head. 'Nothing to repay, and speaking of that, I hope you understand I'll be paying you for the trip. It's not a favour.'

'I don't expect to get paid. You don't have to. I'll enjoy being on the water.' She lifted her eyes and despite herself, she knew her expression was almost coquettish. It was the reaction to his fingers brushing gently on her skin. 'And I'll enjoy getting to know you again, Jake. Find out all about your plans here.'

'And I will too. Enjoy getting to know you.' Jake leaned over and brushed his lips over her cheek and

Jenni froze. Before she could pull back or speak, he'd let her go, and turned to walk back through the gate.

Jenni stood and watched until Jake was at the jetty. He turned back and waved before he disappeared on the deck. She opened the front door and headed to the kitchen. She was wide awake, and her thoughts were in turmoil.

For someone who was here with an ulterior motive, Jake was just *too* nice. He'd welcomed her aboard, he'd shown her around and he'd answered all her questions openly and without hesitation.

The main thing that she'd been wondering about, and that she'd thought was too gauche to ask was where the hell had he got all his money from?

He'd left here ten years ago, with nothing. Now that she'd seen the boat—and there was another one, she realised that Jake's boats were worth millions. They were like nothing that Second Chance Bay had ever seen before.

She went to switch the kitchen light on and jumped as someone moved near the table.

'Oh Mum, you scared me,' she said as the light came on. 'Couldn't you sleep?'

'No. My head was full with what I've got left to do.' Her mother shook her head. 'I heard you go out, and I waited for you to come in. I need to talk to you.'

'Over a cuppa?' Jenni asked with her head on the side.

'Sounds good.'

Jenni stood by the stove as the kettle boiled and she poured the water into the pot. She lifted down two fine china cups and saucers and took the milk from the fridge.

'I've missed you, Jen. Having a natter with the boys over a cup of tea wasn't like having my daughter home. And now you're here, and I'm heading off. Murphy's Law, isn't it?'

Jenni pulled out a chair and sat down and watched as her mother picked up the pot and spun it around before she poured the tea.

'You'll be back before you know it.' A frown creased her forehead. 'Unless Rick wants to stay over there?'

'No, he assures me we'll come back here, as soon as he gets the pub up and running and gets good managers in. This is home. For both of us.'

'So when's the wedding? I hope I get to be bridesmaid.'

'Not for a while. I want to get used to being a part of Rick's life first. By the time we get married, you'll probably have kids who can be page boys and flower girls.'

'That could be a while,' Jenni said as she sipped her tea.

'Am I right in thinking you've been over to see Jake?' Mum's voice was cautious.

Jenni lowered her gaze and nodded. She knew she'd upset Mum when she'd said she was going to find out what Jake was up to.

'He's a good boy, Jen. And I'm very pleased he's done so well for himself.'

Again, she nodded, sipping her tea so she didn't have to answer, but there was no stopping Mum.

'I hope you sorted things with him and you've gotten over this silly idea that Jake is on some sort of vendetta. He doesn't have a dishonest bone in his body, you know.' Mum stared at her and her eyes were intense. 'You do know that, don't you?'

Jenni knew she'd upset Mum enough tonight, so she nodded. 'I do. He's a good man,' she said softly. She was pleased that she did because Mum visibly relaxed. Her shoulders eased and she rested her chin in her hand.

'Oh, that's so good. I can go away and not worry about you. It was making me feel ill, actually. I'm pleased you sorted it out. I hoped he'd tell you the truth.'

Jenni didn't know what her mother was talking about, so she nodded again and then reached for the packet of biscuits in the middle of the table. 'Tim Tam, Mum?'

'Why not? Now tell me all about his boat and where you're going to.'

It was after midnight by the time they stopped chatting, and Jenni smiled as Mum hugged her good night.

'It sounds wonderful, and I'm sure you'll have a fabulous time out there. Text me some photos, won't you?'

'I will. And you send me some of your trip west.'

They walked up the hall together, and Jenni opened her bedroom door. 'Night, Mum. Sleep well.'

'I will now,' her mother said with a smile.

Jenni closed the bedroom door and leaned her back against it.

What a night.

Sitting chatting with Jake as though nothing apart from the role of the hostess was on her mind, and then convincing Mum she didn't have a vendetta going against Jake had been exhausting.

Jenni yawned, but there was one more thing she wanted to do before she went to bed. She crossed to the desk and booted up her laptop, hoping the intermittent internet service was working tonight. Dane and Donny were online gamers, and she could barely get her email to download when they were online. But the house was in darkness, so she assumed they'd gone to bed. The connection was fast and she opened up a search engine and typed in Jake Jones wondering how many there would be in the world.

To her surprise, her Jake—*no, not my Jake*—the Jake she was looking for came up in number one position in the search results.

Jenni read the first article, her eyes widening. By the time she'd scrolled through at least twenty articles, she was even more convinced that Jake was up to something.

And then she searched through the images. A strange feeling settled in her stomach as she flicked through photo after photo of Jake, each time with a different beautiful woman in evening dress on his arm.

She swallowed.

And I sat there tonight on his luxury boat in a pair of faded jeans and a ratty old cardigan.

The bylines under the photos referred to him as the "outback playboy from down under", and "Aussie millionaire" was peppered through some of the articles.

Aussie millionaire!

She kept reading, trying to get some clue as to where Jake had made his money, but there was nothing.

The next page she clicked on was "Exotic Fishing in the Tropics", the tag he'd mentioned tonight. Her eyes almost popped as she went to the booking page and read what the charter fee was per person for a five-day charter.

Almost twenty thousand dollars per angler!

Two hours later, Jenni had exhausted every search avenue. She'd even found Facebook references to Jake in her searching. A photo of Jake in a bar in Monte Carlo, looking no older than when he'd left here. She checked the date; he would have been twenty-two when it was taken.

Me and my deckie mates, the friend who'd posted the photo had tagged it. *Outback Jake.*

A deckie wouldn't have made the money that Jake would have needed to get those two boats. The boats with the fancy china, and the best of everything.

From Outback Jake to Outback playboy.

Jenni dropped her head in her hands.

The only thing she could think of was that Jake had come by his wealth dishonestly. There was no other way he could have afforded those luxurious boats.

Maybe something had happened and he'd fled the Cote d'Azur like he'd left town here.

But why was he here?

Her thoughts went round and round in circles. She threw herself onto her bed and closed her eyes, but her sleep was broken by dreams.

Dreams where Jake was holding her in his arms and telling her he was sorry.

Chapter Thirteen

The night before *Moonshine* and *Starshine* were due to leave on their respective charters, Rick decided to hold an impromptu farewell at the pub. He and Sally were leaving on their trip tomorrow, the same day the charters were heading out into the Gulf.

Not only did Rick invite half the town; he invited Jake and the crew from his boats.

Jake arrived late with Gus; they'd been filling the fuel and water tanks of both boats over at the main dock in town. Then Jake had insisted on a final walk through the two vessels, to make sure that everything was perfect. As they walked along the river to the pub, Gus shook his head.

'Was everything to your satisfaction, *sir*?' His eyes glinted as he chuckled.

Jake nodded. 'It was. There's only one problem.

Gus turned with a frown. 'What?'

'My other skipper is a smart arse.'

Gus laughed as they waited for a space to clear as a crowd jostled to get through the opening in the fence. 'Someone has to keep you in line.' He looked around at the dozens of people under the trees. 'Jeez, this is some big party for a small town.'

Jake shook his head. 'No. Most of these people are tourists here to take photos of the sunset. They'll disappear the instant it drops below the horizon.'

The tiki torches along the edge of the river bank flickered in the early evening breeze as the sun sank lower. Dozens of photographers stood with cameras poised, several even had tripods set up. Gus and Jake waited until there was a gap in the crowd and then Gus pointed to a table at the edge of the open-air bar. 'There's the crew over there.'

The indoor section of the pub was packed, and Jake spotted Rick serving behind the bar as they made their way across to the table.

'Hey, guys.' Jake slid onto the bench seat opposite Claudette, the hostess he'd hired for *Starshine*. It was a small charter world; he'd been pleased when she'd turned up to be interviewed in Darwin. A few years ago, he'd worked with the young Frenchwoman on a charter to Nice, and he knew she had a great work ethic. She'd often mentioned wanting to work in Australia, and during the interview, she'd told Jake she'd followed her dream after a couple of years in the Caribbean. She'd been in Australia for almost a year working in the Whitsundays and had agreed to do Jake's first charter, and then she was flying back to Europe because her visa had expired.

'The French accent will go down well with the clients,' Gus had said when he'd first met Claudette and then he'd winked at Jake. 'Not to mention, she's drop dead gorgeous.'

'She's also an excellent worker,' Jake had said. 'And a top person too. A great sense of humour.'

Gus had sighed. 'My perfect woman.'

'Hey, Jake, Gus.' The two men on the opposite side of the table greeted them both before Gus headed for the bar. Ryan and Cade were both highly experienced deckies who'd come with great references. Ryan had worked out of Darwin, but Cade had worked around the world for different charterers.

'All set for departure tomorrow?' Cade asked.

Jake nodded. 'All good.' He looked around. 'Where's Tony and Jonathon?'

'They're in talking to the chefs in the kitchen. Apparently, there was a delivery of fresh fruit and vegies here today, and they're doing a deal for some extra fresh provisions,' Ryan replied.

Jake leaned back and nodded as Gus put a schooner in front of him. 'Thanks, mate.' He was very satisfied with the crew he'd hired. A chef, a deckie and a hostess for each boat would ensure that the charter ran smoothly. All they needed now was for the guests to fly in tomorrow and his new business would be up and running.

He was nervous. A whole new venture into an area that he was familiar with shouldn't have fazed him, but the investment in setting up the boats and moving to Second Chance Bay had been significant. He'd breathed a sigh of relief when the first two charters had filled within two days of advertising.

'Stop looking so worried, Jake.' Gus held his beer up. 'Cheers, mate, and congratulations on your new venture. It's going to be great.'

'I wish I had your confidence, mate.' Jake stared into his beer and Gus shook his head. 'It's a bit like pre-wedding jitters, isn't it?'

'Who's getting married?'

Jake looked up at Matt who was standing beside him. 'Hi, Matt. No one is. Gus is just giving me a serve because I'm nervous about the first charter.'

'It'll be great. The whole town's talking about it, and how good it is to see you bring your business to town.'

'Really?' Jake moved along so Matt could sit down on his left.

'Yeah. You're a hit already.' Matt put his beer on the table. 'Looks like you've got a top crew too. Your two chefs are in there helping Mum.'

'Helping?'

'Yeah, it's really busy in there and they've both pitched in and helped. Community spirit already.' He looked at Jake with a slight grin. 'You want to watch your new hostess too. One of the chefs was seriously chatting her up in the kitchen.'

Jake looked over at Claudette who was deep in conversation with Ryan and Cade. He frowned. 'My hostess?'

Matt laughed. 'My sister, you boofhead. You know Jenni? Your other hostess.'

'Oh.' Heat rose up Jake's neck. 'Why should I watch her? You mean because there shouldn't be romance between the crew? I've made that clear in the staff procedures. I don't care what happens on shore, but nothing once we're on board.'

Matt shook his head. 'God, you're thick, mate. I meant you had some competition.'

Jake didn't answer for a moment. 'I wish, Matt, but she can't stand me. I was surprised when she agreed to help out.'

'She'll come round. Jenni's done it tough the past few years. She put herself through uni, there was no money when Dad died, and she worked two jobs at night for a few years. Then she's only had contract work since she graduated. Not a bad thing though. I've got a feeling she'll stay here now.'

Jake shook his head. 'She told me she was going back to Brisbane.'

'A bit of self-protection there. She's not as immune to you as she makes out.'

'We'll see.'

'Speak of the devil.' Matt gestured across the bar area. Jenni was making her way over to their table. Jake was pleased; he'd been busy since *Starshine* had arrived and she hadn't been over to meet the crew yet, although it sounded like she'd already met Tony and Jonathon tonight.

He narrowed his eyes; his two chefs who were walking very close to her.

Jake ignored the surge of jealousy that ran through him when Tony reached across and took Jenni's arm. She stopped and turned to him with a wide smile.

Wake up to yourself, he thought. He should be pleased his crew were all getting on well.

Very well, he thought as Jenni's laugh reached them. He hadn't heard that for a long time.

The three were still laughing as they reached the table.

'Hi. Looks like you three have already met.' He moved out from behind the seat and stood next to Jenni. 'Jenni. Meet the rest of the crew. Ryan and Cade are our deckies, and Claudette is the other hostess. And this is Gus.'

As Jenni lifted her hand in a friendly greeting her perfume wafted around him. Despite the cool breeze, it was hot in the crowded area, and she had dressed accordingly. A pretty pink dress draped her soft curves and he was hard-pressed not to stare. Her lips were glossy with some sort of pink stuff, and she'd done something to her eyes, and they looked even wider than usual.

Her cheeks were rosy and her smile wide; he had to concentrate on not reaching out to pull her close to his side. His heart ached for what he'd lost.

Ten years of their lives wasted. All he hoped was that he could convince Jenni that he still loved her, and that he was worth loving back.

He was. And he was going to do his best to convince her of that.

***

Jenni looked at Jake as he sat down and everyone moved along the bench seat so she and the other newcomers could slide in. As she paused, the other places were taken so she had no option but to sit next to him.

Look on it as a positive, she thought; she could see him in action with his crew before the charter began and see what made him tick.

Stupid. I know what makes him tick. I just need to reconcile that with what happened and what he is now.

The conversation was animated and Jenni sat back and let it wash around her.

'So you have the charter route planned, Jake? The weather gods have been kind?' As Jake leaned forward to answer Cade, his leg pressed against Jenni's and she stiffened. She was right on the edge of the seat with no room to slide along, and if she swung to the side, it would be obvious that she was uncomfortable. She sat perfectly still and tried to ignore the little frissons of trembling nerve endings that were firing up with the pressure of Jake's leg against hers.

'Yep. We're going to head out to Sweers Island to start and then we'll head out deep and *Moonshine* will follow the western side of the Gulf over to Limmen Bight. We've got an ornithologist on board who wants to look at the birds there. Gus will head deeper and take the serious fishermen out deep for the last three days.' Jake turned to Jenni. 'I had an enquiry from a scientific group for a similar trip to the bird islands but I've passed that on to Matt. I think your boats could handle the bigger groups.'

'Oh,' she said.

'Yes, I know your brothers haven't ventured away from fishing charters before. There are some great opportunities for scientific trips and some educational government tenders to apply for.'

'I'm sure Matt was pleased.' Jenni smiled but her heart wasn't in it.

Why is Jake so goddamned determined to help my brothers out?

'Yeah. I think he was. We've got to help each other out in this business.'

'That's a generous attitude,' she said carefully as he looked down at her. Jake's eyes were bright and he looked relaxed and happy.

'Jake's always gone out of his way to share his knowledge since I met him.' Gus was looking at them curiously. 'He's done himself out of a bit of business though because he's willing to share.'

'Is that why you came home?' she asked.

'No. I came home for lots of reasons but that wasn't one of them. There was still plenty of work over in the Med.'

She waited for him to elaborate, but Jake turned to Tony. 'When are you loading the supplies onto the boat? The chopper for the first guests for *Moonshine* arrives at ten thirty in the morning. I'd like to have it all stowed by ten at the latest.'

'No problem, boss. Matt and Dane are helping me bring the stuff over from the cool room in the fish shop and Sally's sending the fresh produce over from the pub first thing.'

'Good. 'He nodded. 'Gus, you're all set? Is there anything the crew need to know? If we have a bit of a Q and A now, we can settle back and enjoy the night.'

'No, we're all good. Still embarking at five p.m.?'

'Yep. Tide's good for that.' Jake turned to Jenni. 'Your uniform was okay?'

He'd sent it back with Matt yesterday afternoon. Jenni had tried it on and it had fitted perfectly. Knee-length navy shorts and a white collared shirt with the *Moonshine* logo, as well as a cap with *Moonshine* embroidered on the brim. Jake had also sent a message to say any colour white-soled shoes would be fine.

'Yes. All good. What time do you want me there tomorrow?'

'Sorry, I thought I'd already told you that. If you can be there at eight, Claudette will take you through the procedures for meeting and greeting and getting the guests settled. We'll give them lunch on board, and then Cade will do some fishing talks in the afternoon.'

A tendril of excitement began to unfurl in Jenni's chest. If only she was going on this trip purely to work. Without her ulterior motive of sussing Jake and his motives out, she could really enjoy the week. It had been a long time since she'd gone out on a charter. When she was in her mid-teens, Dad had let her go on a couple of fishing charters on *Elsie.*

In the days when Dad had been happier and hadn't carried that dark look and bad mood on his shoulders.

Now that she was an adult and knew the financial difficulties that a business could face, she could understand more why Dad had changed. The financial pressures must have become burdensome. All she could remember was Mum looking worried, and Dad spent a lot of time at the pub in town. It had been a relief to leave and head to Brisbane to get away from the tense atmosphere, especially when Jake had left, and she no longer had anyone to talk to about the situation.

When he'd been out on the water, Dad had been happy. He knew where the fish were—the locals used to say the McDougals could smell the fish on the wind and knew where to go to get the best catch. That was one of the reasons their charters had been the most popular back in the early days.

Jenni swallowed as the excitement dissipated and a heavy sadness settled in her chest.

Why was she doing this? Mum was about to leave and the boys were doing okay. She should just go back to Brisbane and pick up her old life.

Jenni jumped as Jake's breath warmed her cheeks as he leaned closer and spoke quietly.

'You okay, Jen? You're not worried about working on the boat, are you?'

She shook her head but as she went to speak the noise of the conversations rose around them.

'Too noisy,' she mouthed back.

Jake nodded to the shore. 'Come for a walk with me.'

Reluctance warred with her desire to go with Jake, but it would have looked strange if she'd refused. Jenni slid out of the bench seat and waited for Jake to follow. He led the way past the low fence and the coastal almond trees. The sun was hovering over the horizon and a burst of golden light spread over the dark blue water. The red and green channel lights flickered in the distance and the lights of the McDougal croc tour boat winked as it headed back to the dock. Dane and Donny had taken an early tour out tonight so they could get back for Mum and Rick's farewell.

They reached the sand and stood looking over the water. After a moment of silence, Jake reached out and took Jenni's hand and she caught her breath.

'Is everything okay, Jenni? You looked really worried back there. You'll be fine.' He chuckled. 'I'm not a hard taskmaster, and anything you need to know, just ask me.'

'No, I'm looking forward to it.' She decided to be honest with him, it wouldn't hurt. 'I was thinking about when I used to go out with Dad on the charters when we were in high school. Back in the good old days.'

Jake dropped her hand and turned back to look at the water. 'Yeah, the good old days.'

She was surprised to hear the cynical tone in his voice. Before she could answer, the PA system crackled and Rick's voice came over the speakers.

'I'd like to welcome everyone here tonight. After dinner, I've got some thank yous to make and we've got some celebrating to do, and I'd like to get my lovely lady out of the kitchen sooner than later, so if you haven't ordered your meal yet, please come on up and place your orders now.'

'Come on.' Jenni turned to go back but Jake's hand fell gently on her shoulder. She turned back slowly. His face was in the shadows, his head silhouetted by the great orange ball of sun on the horizon.

'Wait.' His voice was soft. 'Watch the sunset with me first. Like we used to.'

'No, Jake. We need to order. Rick wants Mum out of the kitchen.' Her voice was harsh. If Jake had taken her in his arms and counted down the sunset with her, Jenni knew she would have cried.

Cried for what they had lost, and for what they had become.

She turned on her heel and left him on the sand, watching the sun slip below the horizon—alone.

Chapter Fourteen

Despite being confident that she could handle the hostess work, Jenni wiped her hands nervously on her shorts as Jake turned *Moonshine* towards the main dock in town. He'd been quiet since Claudette had gone back to *Starshine* and both boats had left the dock at Second Chance Bay and headed to the port in town. The smaller boat was following *Moonshine* along the river.

Jenni had checked the guest rooms, set the tables for lunch, and put the fresh flowers that had been delivered onboard this morning into each of the cabins, as well as the saloon and the dining areas. As they approached the public dock, her eyes widened. A small crowd of people stood next to a minibus with the *Moonshine* and *Starshine* logos sign written on the side, along with a background of blue water and jumping fish.

A bus just for the short trip from the airport three hundred metres away? *Just how rich was Jake?*

The playboy description she'd seen on the internet and the pictures of him in evening dress came back into her mind. She'd been softening towards him ever since her harsh dismissal of him at sunset last night. Guilt had rippled through all her night and she hadn't slept well. It had lasted through the speeches Rick had made, through the congratulations to the older couple of=n their engagement, and when Mum had come up and hugged her and wished her a good trip.

When Mum had turned to Jake and hugged him, she'd heard her say, 'Look after my girl.'

Dane and Donny and Matt had been in fine form, and each of them had bought Jake a beer until he'd held up his hand and said, 'soda water for me for the rest of the night. I'm skippering tomorrow.'

Why is it only me who can see Jake for what he is?

Why was the rest of her family falling over themselves to be nice to him, and to listen to all of his suggestions?

Mum had hugged her tight this morning after they'd shared a pot of tea at daybreak in time for Jenni to walk over to the boat.

'You look nice in your uniform, love.'

'Thanks. I look the part anyway,' she replied with a laugh. Matt poked his head around the door with a yawn. 'How long till you both leave?'

'I'm going in ten minutes,' Jenni replied.

'Rick's picking me up at seven.' Mum lifted the pot. 'Want a cuppa?'

Matt nodded. 'I'll tell Dane and Donny you're both about to go.'

Sitting at the kitchen table with Mum, and her three brothers in their PJs made Jenni smile, even though she knew Mum was heading a few thousand kilometres away from them. After the pot was drained and almost a whole loaf of bread had been toasted and demolished by her brothers, Jenni stood. Her small bag was packed and waiting by the door.

'Enjoy yourself, pipsqueak,' Matt said. Donny and Dane echoed his comment, with their mouths full.

'Enjoy cleaning those fish,' Donny said.

She dropped a kiss on the top of his head as she walked past. 'I do it better than you anyway.'

Mum had followed her outside and held her arms out for a hug. 'You have a great time, darling. And Jenni, can I ask you just one thing?'

Jenni smiled and nodded. 'Of course.'

'You be nice to Jake, okay?'

She'd nodded jerkily.

'Cake's out of the oven.' Tony's voice interrupted her thoughts and she forced a smile to her face. She'd been disappointed when she'd realised Tony was the chef on *Moonshine;* he'd been a little bit too friendly and familiar last night, and she hoped he knew that once they were on board, there was a rule for staff behaviour.

'Thanks. I've got the coffee pots on and the table's set for lunch. The coffee tables are ready for morning tea to be served.'

'Interesting mix of guests.' Tony nodded to the wharf as Cade jumped off the bow and secured the ropes to the bollards. He waited there until *Starshine* eased in on the other side of the dock and secured her ropes too.

Jake helped Cade lift the gangplank down before he walked onto the jetty. Jenni watched as he shook the hands of the men, and smiled as he took the hands of the only two female guests who stood at the back of the group. For a moment she thought he was going to kiss their hands, and she smothered a laugh. He wasn't that European.

'I'm looking forward to the charter,' Jenni replied. 'I hope they're not too hard to please.'

'If you have any problems, don't hesitate to ask. I'm happy to help you with anything.'

She went to say thank you, but then Tony added. 'You know where my cabin is.'

She nodded briskly. 'If I have any questions, I'm sure Jake will be happy to answer them. He's already offered.'

Tony's eyebrows rose. 'Whoops, am I poaching on the captain's territory?'

Jenni held his gaze and didn't confirm or deny his assumption. It might make life easier if Tony thought that she was involved with Jake. Everyone knew they'd known each other for a long time. She walked to the deck where the gangplank joined the boat and watched as Jake directed the guests to the respective vessels. Claudette was standing at the top of the gang plank on *Starshine* and she gave Jenni a wide smile as the first guests headed to each boat.

Jake walked ahead of them and Jenni stood back as the six guests for *Moonshine* boarded. Tony and Cade came and stood beside her.

'Welcome aboard everyone. I'd like you to meet our lovely hostess, Jenni, our fabulous chef, Tony, and you've already seen our deckhand, Cade in action. Because we're such a small group, there's no need for name tags.' Jake turned to the crew. 'I'd like to introduce our guests to you.'

Jenni put her hands behind her back. For some silly reason, her hands were shaking as Jake did his professional spiel; he had a commanding presence.

'Professor Jim Ramsey, and his wife, Leonora.' The professor and his wife smiled as Jake introduced them.

'And this is Greg Saunders, Pat Andrews, Alan Ward, and last but not least, Ken Erikson.'

As the four men returned the greeting, Jake stepped back. 'I'm off to the wheelhouse now. Jenni will show you to your cabins, and then morning tea will be served. I'll be back down to join you for any questions you may have.' He glanced at Jenni and she nodded.

She'd familiarised herself with the cabins that had been allocated and stepped up to the professor and his wife. 'If you'd like to follow me, I'll show you to your cabins first. Cade has already put your bags in there for you.'

Once the guests had been shown to their various cabins—each of the men had been allocated a single cabin—meaning Jenni had five cabins to service twice a day, she hurried back to the saloon. Tony had put a plate of warm scones covered with a tea towel on each coffee table along with single plates of freshly made carrot cake with cream on the side.

'Yum, smells great,' Jenni said as she checked the coffee pot.

'There's plates served out in the galley for you and Cade. The captain will have his with the guests. Come and have it now, you've got time for a quick cuppa before they come up.'

Jenni grabbed a coffee and hurried to the galley, one eye out for the appearance of the first guest. Tony took her through the procedure for the serving of the cold platters for lunch and she was pleased to note his new professional distance.

As long as he doesn't say anything to Jake about thinking that he and the new hostess were an item.

Leonora Ramsey walked along the deck past the open galley window. Jenni drained her coffee, dabbed at her mouth with a serviette and hurried to the door. 'Great cake, thanks Tony.'

***

Jake watched as Jenni served and cleared away lunch. Her movements were deft, and she was professional as she engaged the guests in friendly conversation. After the guests left the dining tables to go back to their cabins, he sought her out in the galley. His eyes narrowed as he stood at the door. Jenni and Tony were standing close to each other, deep in conversation. Her smile was wide and natural as she looked up at the chef, and Jake waited until she went back to the sink before he walked in.

He injected a bright note into his voice. 'Thanks, both of you. Great lunch, and nicely served.'

'Thanks, captain. Would you like to look at the menu for dinner? I was just showing Jenni which wines to chill.'

Jake shook his head. 'No need. I have every confidence it will be excellent, thanks Tony.' If there was one thing he knew was important, it was to show his crew he had confidence in them.

Tony nodded and went back to the cool room.

'Jenni. Could you come up to the wheelhouse for a moment?'

Jake was angry at himself. It was stupid to be jealous because Jenni was talking to Tony. She was simply doing her job, but he couldn't handle the thought of her being interested in someone else. It was something he was going to have to get over, because if anything, the longer he'd been in town, Jenni's attitude to him had cooled even more. He stepped back and gestured for her to precede him and followed her up the polished timber stairs to the top deck.

'Have a seat, please.' He pointed to the second swivel seat next to his.

'Is there something wrong, captain?'

His eyes narrowed at her tone. It was very different to the friendly way she'd been speaking to Tony a few minutes ago.

'No. I just wanted to check that you were on top of everything, Jenni. Any questions? Problems? You know what you have to do for the rest of the day?'

Jake stared past her to the jetty.

Jeez, he was going about this the wrong way.

'Yes. I'm fine. Claudette was thorough. I know where everything is, and I know what needs to be done.' She lifted her face to his and a glimmer of a smile appeared. 'In fact, I don't think I'm going to be very busy, am I? Once the cabins are serviced in the mornings, there's not a lot left for me to do apart from the meals.'

Jake let himself grin. 'You could help Cade with the fish filleting.'

'If there's any fish caught.'

'Don't you worry about that. My charters will be renowned for the fish we catch.' The atmosphere lightened as Jenni's laugh filled the wheelhouse.

'Don't tell me the boys taught you how to smell the fish out?'

Jake shook his head. 'No, I have to be honest. Today's technology is probably better than that.' He pointed to the large screen of a state-of-the-art fish finder on the console.

'That's cheating.' Jenni shook her head. 'Not as good as the old ways.'

'I guess I have to agree, and that's why I want to support the boys with your charter boats. There's a lot of fishermen who prefer to chase the fish without modern technology.'

Her expression clouded for a fleeting moment, before she looked back at him. Her voice was low and intense. 'Don't get me wrong, Jake. I appreciate what you seem to want to do.'

Seem to. He lifted his chin and waited for her to continue.

'You seem so keen to help the boys build our charter business back up.'

He nodded.

'But what I don't get is why you would want to?'

Jake kept his voice controlled. They were getting too close to what he didn't want Jenni to know. 'Can't the why just be that I want to share my skills with people that I grew up with? Men who I respect and admire? Men who taught me a lot over the years before I left?'

The last three words hung in the air between them. Jake would never tell Jenni why he'd left town. If she ever came to trust him, it would be without knowing why he had.

He didn't want to burden her with the truth.

Chapter Fifteen

The sun was low in the sky as *Moonshine* left the dock and led the way to the river mouth and the two motor cruisers made their way out into the Gulf. Jake slowed down each time one of the mosquito fleet boats came in through the heads so the wash of the cruiser didn't reach the small boats. Jenni stood on the bow and waved as they passed the sand bar where Dane and Donny had a full complement of guests out watching the sunset. As they waved back, Jake tooted the horn above. Their guests were all up on the top deck with their cameras.

Jenni moved back to the saloon. As soon as the sun slipped out of sight it was time to serve the pre-dinner drinks and canapés that Tony was preparing in the galley. As she hurried around to the passageway that ran along from the bow to the stern, she caught her breath as Jake's hands grabbed her shoulders before she ran into him.

'Sorry, I wasn't watching where I was going.'

'All good. I saw you back there. I was coming down to watch the sunset with you.'

Heat rose up Jenni's neck as Jake's hands continued to hold her gently.

His voice was low. 'We need to get this sunset watching organised. I'm not going to give up, you know, Jen.'

She frowned at his enigmatic words. 'Give up on what, Jake?'

'Convincing you to watch a sunset with me.'

She shook herself from his grasp and pointed to the sun as it hovered above the horizon. 'I'm here, you're here. The sun is setting. You can't get more organised than that. Excuse me, Jake. I have canapés to put out.'

Jenni's breath caught as Jake's fingers tightened and he looked around. The guests were up top, Tony was in the kitchen and there was no sign of Cade. He lowered his head closer to hers and before she could step back, his lips brushed her cheek, just above the corner of her lips.

Jenni put her fingers to her cheek as he stepped away.

'Now we're organised. And I'm happy. Think about that, Jen.'

Before she could answer, Jake turned and hurried back to the wheelhouse, where he'd obviously left Cade.

She was thoughtful as she walked to the saloon. Maybe that was the way to find out what he was up to.

Respond a little bit, and get his trust.

Jenni nodded. It couldn't hurt as a strategy.

And it could be pleasant, said the little voice deep in her heart.

##

Dinner was a noisy affair. The more wine Jenni served, the louder a couple of the younger customers became. Ken and Greg insisted on tipping Jenni each time she poured a glass of wine for them, and there were several of those poured before it was time to serve dessert. She hurried into the galley with the cleared dishes from the main course.

'Tony, do you have a spare jar or a plastic container?'

'Sure.' He opened a cupboard next to the cool room and passed her a tall plastic jar with a red screw top lid. Jenni dug into her pocket and pulled out the six fifty-dollar notes that had been slipped to her during dinner.

She shook her head as embarrassment flooded her. 'I'm not used to this tipping business. It really makes me uncomfortable.'

'It's the way the charters work, sweetheart. All over the world, so don't be embarrassed. It's an endorsement of the great job you're doing. You should know that.'

'It's an indication of how much they're drinking. I feel like giving it back to them in the morning,' she said with a rueful smile as she dropped the notes into the jar and screwed the lid tight.

'Surely you're used to being tipped?' Tony asked as he added a scoop of ice cream to each bowl and then put a fresh mint leaf on top.

Jenni shook her head as she put the jar back into the cupboard. 'This is the first commercial charter

I've done at this level of luxury. Or should I say with this level of client. I'm used to working on my family's boats.' She didn't see the need to tell him she was actually a teacher, and doing a favour for Jake.

'Just do the job and smile. I think that younger pair are "fly in fly out" miners. I heard them talking on the deck before. They'll be single and have plenty of disposable income.'

Jenni sighed as she picked up the first two desserts that Tony had plated to take into the dining room. 'I'll try to get used to it.'

The two men were speaking loudly as she placed the dessert plates in front of the professor and his wife. As she turned to go back to the galley for the rest of the desserts, Jake walked down the staircase from the upper deck and glanced over to where the two young men were getting louder.

Jenni paused. 'Would you like your dinner served now, captain?'

Jake turned and held her gaze steadily. 'That would be good, thank you, Jenni.'

As he walked out, she noticed that he went to sit at the table were the two young guys were sitting. The other two older fishermen were sitting with the professor and Leonora.

She asked Tony to serve Jake's dinner and then loaded up four dessert plates and headed back to the dining table, pleased to hear that the conversations had returned to a normal conversational level of sound, as Jake steered the conversation to the fishing tomorrow. When she placed the dessert in front of Ken, he reached into his pocket and she held up a hand.

'No, thank you. It's fine. My pleasure.' She hurried out of the room and back to the kitchen, but caught Jake's frown as she turned to the door.

'Jake's dinner is right to go,' Tony said.

'I'll be straight back for it.' Jenni said as she picked up the last two desserts. 'But I think I'm trouble.'

Tony looked at her curiously. 'What did you do?

'I held up my hand and said not necessary when Ken went to pull out another note for another bloody tip.'

'Customer is always right, sweetheart.' Tony flicked a tea towel over his shoulder.

As she picked up the desserts, Jake's cold voice reached her. 'Tony's right. The customer is always right. What was that all about? The 'it's my pleasure.'

Temper began to simmer in Jenni's chest. Less than twenty-four hours on the boat and she was already regretting it. With her mouth set, she put the plates down, and strode to the cupboard, pulled out the jar and held it up.

'This is what it was all about, *captain*. It mightn't bother you if *customers* want to throw fifty-dollar notes away—three hundred dollars' worth in one meal—but it sure bothers me. If this is what luxury cruising is, you can give me the *Sally M* charter any day.'

While she stood there and eyeballed Jake, Tony disappeared into the cool room.

'I'm sorry. I can understand why you feel uncomfortable. That's a bit over the top.'

'Do you really think that, or are you just saying it to make yourself look better, Jake? It's all about the money for you, isn't it?' Jenni's voice rose in volume and pitch. 'Well, you know what? I don't think the McDougal family needs that sort of help.'

Jake's eyes widened and a dark flush stained his cheeks. 'We'll talk about this later. I'll take my dinner in and you bring the rest of the desserts. They'll be waiting for them.' He waited for her to pick up the desserts before he came into the galley. Jenni had to brush past him on the way out and she could feel the tension in his body. She looked up and could see a muscle twitching in his cheek.

Jake picked up his dinner and by the time he followed her into the dining room, he was smiling and his body was at ease.

Even his body can lie, she thought.

Four more nights.

Four more nights of putting up with Jake Jones and his bloody boat.

Chapter Sixteen

Jake waited until the guests had left the dining room and headed out to the deck. Professor Ramsey and his wife had declined the offer of coffee; they were going to have an early night, but the other four had decided to have a night fish as soon as *Moonshine* stopped travelling.

'We'll pull up for an hour or two,' Jake said. 'I'll send Cade down to rig the lines for you after I go up to the wheelhouse.' He would have preferred to travel a bit further, but as he'd told Jenni earlier, the customer was always right and they were here to please. The weather forecast was good—no wind—so they might as well take advantage of the calm conditions and fish while they could. 'I'll get Jenni to bring your coffee out to you on the deck. A rule on my charter, guys, no drinking on deck while you fish. It's not safe.'

Jake went back to the galley. Tony and Jenni were talking quietly but stopped and looked up as soon as he appeared in the doorway.

'Coffee for the guys out on deck, please, Jenni. They're going to fish for a while. No more alcohol to be served tonight. When you do that, can you bring me a coffee up to the wheelhouse please. Black with two sugars.'

Jenni nodded and turned her attention back to the sink.

'You can knock off after that. The coffee cups can be brought in when you set up for breakfast in the morning.'

'Okay, I'll be up in ten. I'll just finish up here, if that's all right?' She lifted her chin and met his gaze steadily, but her cheeks were tinged with pink.

Jake nodded. 'That's fine. Take as long as you like. I'll be up there for a few hours.'

Jenni frowned. 'All night?'

'No. Cade will take over at midnight. We should be at Sweers Island by then.'

He went up the wheelhouse using the outside stairs so he could check on the two younger men on the way. They'd sobered up a bit once the fresh salty air had hit them, and the four men were sitting quietly on the fishing deck on the stern.

'Good luck fishing, guys. If you'd like your catch cooked fresh or frozen down to take home, we can do either. Just let Cade know your preference. He'll look after you.' Once he was confident they were all fit enough to be safely out on deck, Jake ran up the stairs and relieved Cade.

'We're pulling up to fish for an hour. We'll anchor here; it's not real deep so we won't need much chain.'

'Rightio, skipper,' Cade said. 'I'll head out to the bow. Are you ready now?'

Jake nodded. 'Yep, give me five to check the radar and call *Starshine*.'

He checked the radar and made sure they weren't in a shipping passage, and once he was sure it was clear around them, he radioed Gus and explained they were pulling up to fish for an hour.

'We're about two nautical miles behind you, boss. I think we'll keep going. We've got a quiet group on here. They all went to their cabins after dinner.'

'A bit of a rowdy crew here, but harmless. Like throwing their money around, though. Cashed-up miners.' He looked up as there was a movement in the doorway. Jenni was standing there with a mug of coffee in her hand. She went to put it on the table and leave but Jake held up his hand for her to wait.

'I'll call you in the morning to see where you are. Forecast is looking good, and there's not many boats out here.'

'Roger, boss. Over and out.'

He hung up the radio mike and swung around on his chair. 'Thanks for the coffee, Jen. Appreciate it.'

She nodded and stood there quietly.

'Oh, for goodness' sake, stop looking at me as though I'm the devil incarnate.' Jake ran his hand over his head in frustration and closed his eyes for a minute. When he opened them, Jenni was sitting on the chair next to his, staring ahead out to sea.

'Just wait there while Cade puts the anchor out. We need to talk.'

He cut the engines and waited for the boat to stop, and then he stood and signalled to Cade. The deckie released the brake on the gypsy and the anchor chain rattled out. Jake watched the depth indicator and indicated with hand signals to Cade when enough chain was out. Finally, Cade locked off the brake and put the devil's claw on a chain link. He stood there for a moment, one foot on the chain feeling the tension until the anchor took hold and then he gave Jake a thumbs up.

'Thanks, mate,' Jake said when Cade came to the wheelhouse door. 'Four of the guests are waiting on the aft deck for you. Just an hour's fishing, and then get some sleep. I'll see you at midnight. We might do some drift fishing tomorrow if it's quiet.'

Jenni sat there quietly, but when he turned from the door, Jake noticed she was looking at the instrument panel.

'You haven't forgotten what the fishing is like out here then?' she said.

At least she was talking to him.

'No. Once learned never forgotten.'

'What was it like in the Mediterranean?' Her voice sounded interested, and Jake didn't think she was just filling in time.

'Why do you ask?'

'Just interested.' Now her voice was wary as though she'd overstepped some hidden mark.

'The fishing, or the work, or just being there?'

'All of the above, I guess.'

Jake sat on his chair and ran a quick eye over the instruments before he spoke. 'An honest answer?'

'Yes please.'

'It was lonely to start with, and then it was bloody hard work.'

'To start with?'

He nodded. 'After the first three years, and they were hard years, I got used to it. Mum died, and I couldn't afford to come home. I didn't think I'd ever—'

Jesus. He must be tired; he'd almost said he'd never forgive her father for running him out of town.

'Ever what, Jake?' Her voice was soft.

'Ever forget not being here for Mum when she was sick.'

'It would have been hard. I was away when Dad had his heart attack too. I never got to say goodbye.'

'I'm sorry.' Jake leaned forward and took one of Jenni's hands between his. 'Jen?'

'Yes?'

'Can we start again? Can we forget everything that's happened and just pretend that we are getting to know each other now? Let the past go?'

'Maybe.' Her eyes were downcast, and the lights from the instrument panel flickered over her face in a macabre shadow.

'I'm sorry I was short with you over that tipping business. It's been a while since I've had to deal with something like that, and I didn't handle it well. I'll have a word with them if it's making you uncomfortable.'

'With the cashed-up miners?'

He detected a note of disbelief in her voice, but he nodded. 'Yes.'

'If that's what you want. I thought that you'd want as much money out of this charter as you could get.'

Jake looked at her and he wrinkled his brow in a frown. 'Why would you think that? The tips go to the staff. Usually, we pool them and divvy them up at the end. Or that's what happened in Monte Carlo. This is my first trip out here, remember.'

'Tell me more about your time over there. Did you ever get to Paris?'

'I did. It's a beautiful city.'

'One day,' she said softly. 'Now tell me why you really left?'

'Left there, or left here?' He stared at her but she wouldn't meet his eye. 'I'll never forget not being able to talk to you before I left Second Chance Bay.'

She lifted her head. 'Your actions decided your path, Jake.'

'I guess I'll always be guilty to you then.' Weariness flooded through him. 'We've got a big day tomorrow. Go to bed.'

He couldn't even bring himself to her name. Without another word, or even a glance in his direction she picked up his empty coffee mug and left.

Jake stared out over the sea for ages. The moon had risen and a silver path danced on the low waves. The occasional whoop from the aft deck indicated that there were fish being caught but after an hour, the noise stopped as Cade wound up the fishing.

He decided to stay on the anchorage until dawn; he was in no mood to look for uncharted reefs. It wouldn't matter if they arrived at Sweers Island a few hours after *Starshine*. Picking up the mike, he called Gus so he wouldn't worry when they weren't behind them.

The night was quiet; there was nothing apart from the slap of the waves on the hull and the clank of the anchor chain on the bow. The current gurgled quietly as it rushed past the hull, mirroring the thoughts that rushed through Jake's head. But unlike the current, they had no direction.

How the hell had he ever thought bringing Jenni on the boat was going to put him in a better light?

From her attitude tonight, it was obvious that he'd been judged and found wanting.

Jake dropped his head in his hands as he sat out the watch until Cade came to relieve him at midnight. The sad part was, no matter how Jenni looked at him or how she reacted to him, he couldn't stop caring about her. He knew underneath that cynical exterior was the young girl he'd fallen in love with. Hell, he was even more attracted to the feisty woman she was now.

The question was: what could he do about it? He shook his head as the night closed in around him.

There was nothing he could do.

The only thing that would convince her that he was a decent guy was to tell her the truth about her father and what he'd done, but that would destroy any chance of them ever being together.

Shit, what had been the point of him coming home?

Maybe he'd pack up the boats and head back to France.

At least he was respected there for what he'd achieved.

Chapter Seventeen

Jenni lay in her bunk in the cabin on the bottom deck and sleep eluded her. The sadness in Jake's voice and the despair in his expression had almost brought her undone. She couldn't understand him. He had what he wanted; what more could he want?

Why did he look and sound so unhappy? After an hour the rocking of the boat in the gentle swell hadn't helped her get to sleep. She lay there wide-awake staring at the moonlight playing across the ceiling.

No matter what had happened in the past, she had to forgive Jake. Seeing him so unhappy was awful; she couldn't cope with it. From tomorrow, she'd change her attitude and be kind to him.

At least she could do the right thing. Watching Jake and trying to figure him out wasn't going to work. Her feelings for him were still there. Okay, they were hidden under years of resentment and bitterness, but the more time she spent with him, the more that was rolling away. She'd never met anyone else who made her feel like he did, no one else who she worried about when they were sad.

I guess that's what love is, she thought, finally admitting it to herself.

She'd loved him when he'd left and that was why it had left such a mark on her soul. And she still loved Jake Jones.

Tomorrow was a new day. There were four days ahead to get themselves sorted.

Jenni rolled over and thumped her pillow, but there was a smile on her face as she drifted off to sleep.

***

Just after dawn at first light, the engines fired and Jenni woke as the boat began to move. She pulled over her phone and looked at the time; it was almost five thirty and she had plenty of time before she was due up in the galley. She lay there for a moment and then decided to get up. Maybe Jake was back in the wheelhouse; she knew from her time on Dad's boat that a watch was not supposed to be more than four hours. She smiled; Jake would follow the rules; she had no doubt of that.

With a smile, and feeling happier than she had since she'd come back to Second Chance Bay and first seen Jake, Jenni climbed out of the bunk and had a quick shower in the small bathroom attached to her cabin. She pulled out a clean shirt and gathered yesterday's clothes to run through the washing machine, reminding herself to offer to wash the rest of the crew's clothes. Yesterday's desire to leave the boat and go back home had gone, and the day ahead beckoned with promise.

But her smile didn't last long after she arrived on the top deck. Jake was in the wheelhouse and when she waved good morning, he scowled and turned his head away. Okay, she could cope with that; she'd been in a similar mood for a week or more.

Leonora Ramsey was already in the saloon, and Jenni quickly gathered up the tray of coffee cups that the fishermen had left on the table.

'Good morning,' she said with a bright smile. 'Can I get you a coffee, Mrs Ramsey?'

'Leonora, please, and that would be great, thank you.'

'I won't be long.'

Tony was already in the kitchen chopping up fresh fruit for a fruit salad. 'Morning, sunshine,' he said. 'You look bright and happy this morning. You must have slept well.'

'I did, actually,' she said. 'Before I forget, throw your clothes into the hamper up on the main deck, and I'll put them through the machine and dryer for you.'

'Thanks, sweets. Can you do me a favour if you're going that way?'

'Sure,' Jenni nodded as she got the coffee machine going. 'What do you need?'

'Do you know where the lazerette is?'

'Yes, the bit up the front under the wheelhouse?'

'Yep. Aft of the wheelhouse,' he said with a smile.' If you're up that way, there's a big bag of muesli just inside the door. Could you be a love and grab it for me?'

'I'll just wait for the coffee to perk and I'll take one up to Jake if he's still up there.'

'I'd say he will be because young Cade was snoring fairly well in the cabin next to me when I came past. They stick rigidly to their four-hour watches by the look of things. Jake is a good skipper.'

Jenni grinned.

Good, the first chance to make amends to Jake.

She poured two coffees and took one into the saloon to Leonora with a small dish of pastries. 'Breakfast will be on in an hour or so. This should keep you going.'

Leonora looked up from the bird book she was reading. 'Thank you.'

Jenni carefully navigated the stairs as she carried up Jake's coffee.

Black with two.

The sea was a little rougher today and she hung onto the rail with one hand as she went up to the top deck. As she stepped out of the stairwell, she looked ahead. They were approaching a small island. Whitecaps dotted the sea between the boat and the land, and it rocked slightly in the long lazy swells that were under the short choppy waves.

'Morning, captain,' she said brightly.

Jake turned and his face was set. 'Thank you, just leave it on the table.' He turned away and Jenni stood there for a moment before she realised he wasn't going to say any more than that.

With a shrug, she looked around trying to remember where the hatch was that led to the lazerette storage area Jake had shown her the night he had taken her on the tour of the boat. She leaned forward and looked past the wheelhouse but couldn't see it. Finally, he turned.

'Was there something else?'

'Um, the storage area? You showed me a hatch that led to it the other night?'

'Down on the aft deck.' His voice was short and he turned back to the instrument panel.

'Thank you,' Jenni muttered heading back to the stairway.

She found the hatch, retrieved the muesli and delivered it to Tony. By the time she had a load of washing on, and returned to the galley, the appetising aroma of bacon and eggs filled the middle deck.

'I'll just set the tables.' She hurried into the dining area, and quickly laid out the cutlery and plates.

Just as well I got up early, she thought. Being a hostess was a lot more time-consuming then she'd thought it would be. But Jenni was enjoying it so far today, despite Jake's bad mood.

Meal preparation on the *Sally M* and the *Elsie* had been a lot more casual—more along the lines of every man for himself. But then she reminded herself that guests on her brothers' boat didn't pay the exorbitant price that guests were paying on *Moonshine*.

A tendril of doubt began to unfurl and she pushed it away. Today was the day to give Jake another chance. She swallowed and carried the meals into the dining room. Everyone was quiet this morning, and the men barely noticed her, apart from a quick nod of thanks as she put the plates on the table.

No stupid tips this morning, she thought thankfully.

Breakfast was served and cleared away quickly as the island approached. Not far away, *Starshine* was moored on their port side.

Professor Ramsey, and his wife had opted to go ashore and Cade was taking them in the rubber tender. The other four men were fishing off the aft deck, and Jake had come down from the wheelhouse once the anchor was set.

'When you get the cabins serviced and after morning tea, I'll get you to give me a hand down here, please.'

She nodded and hurried off. If it put Jake in a better and more approachable mood, she was happy to help with the fishing. By the time the beds were made, the washing was in the dryer and the bathrooms wiped over, it was morning tea time.

Cade had returned in the tender and was helping out on the aft deck, rigging lines, and baiting hooks. When Jenni went to the aft deck after morning tea had been brought out, and then tidied up, Jake shook his head. 'It's fine. We don't need you now. Cade's back.'

She got the impression that she had taken longer than he'd expected but was determined not to let it worry her; she was here as a hostess and she was doing the duties as directed. Heading to the galley, she poked her head in to see if Tony needed a hand with anything but he wasn't in there. With a shrug, she headed back to the dryer and took the clothes out and folded them, and then put them in the crew cabins.

When she came out there was a lot of noise down on the fishing deck. Curiosity got the better of her, and Jenni ran lightly down the stairs. She stopped at the bottom in time to see Ken's rod bent double and him digging his heels into the deck as the momentum of whatever was on the end of his rod pulled him forward.

Jake looked over and saw her and the smile that crossed his face was spontaneous. Jenni grinned back.

'Can you give us a hand now, Jen?' he called across the deck. 'We've got a bit of a tangle down the back on the lower deck and we need to clear it before the fish goes around there.'

Jenni let her gaze follow to where Jake was pointing. Greg and Pat had their lines tangled and the final mess was tangled around the railing on the starboard side. She nodded and gave Jake a thumbs up, and hurried down to the lower deck. As she leaned over the railing and reached for the tangled line, she heard the tender. Cade had collected Professor Ramsey and Leonora from the island and was approaching the cruiser.

Everything happened at once. The huge fish that was pulling Ken's line headed beneath the back of the boat, and the calls from the upper deck were louder as he fought to keep it. As Jenni watched the line bobbing in the choppy waves, a couple of black fins cruised between the approaching tender and the back of the boat as the sharks picked up the frantic movements of the fish as it fought for its life.

'There it is!' Ken's voice was loud as she stood there holding the tangled lines and looking up, and the silver glint of a massive northern blue fin tuna broke the surface briefly before it headed back under the water. As Ken disappeared around the port side of the boat, she caught a glimpse of two more large sharks hanging around.

Game fishing at its best.

Jenni had forgotten how much she enjoyed being out on the water and seeing the thrill of the catch. The fishermen would be happy. She climbed over onto the duckboard at the back of the boat as the tender approached. By the smiles on the Ramseys' faces, it looked as though the bird watching trip had been successful too. Catching Cade's attention, she pointed up to the fishing deck and he nodded and throttled back the small outboard. After a minute of idling at the back of the boat, Jake called over.

'All clear now.'

Cade gunned the outboard, and when they reached the back of *Moonshine*, he threw the rope to Jenni. The waves were getting choppier as the wind picked up.

Professor Ramsey stood and jumped onto the duckboard next to Jenni as the tender bobbed in the waves. Cade held his hand out for Leonora to take hold and Jenni leaned forward ready to help her on board. As she stepped out of the tender, a large rolling swell caught the tender and slewed it to the side.

Jenni watched in horror as the woman slipped between the tender and the back of the boat, and disappeared into the oily dark water.

Without a second thought, she kicked off her canvas shoes and dived into the water, aware of Cade reversing the tender away from the boat.

Trying not to think of the sharks that she'd seen only a few moments ago, she dived beneath the back of the cruiser and opened her eyes. The current was strong and the salt water stung her eyes. She trod water and looked around. Leonora was already about five metres away from the back of the boat.

Jenni pushed to the surface and pointed to where Leonora was trying to swim against the current. 'Cade, she's over there and drifting away! Quick!' she yelled.

Taking another deep breath, she dived beneath the water.

Chapter Eighteen

Jake's blood turned to ice as Jennie disappeared beneath *Moonshine*. He knew she was a strong swimmer and that she was confident in the water, but she had a huge vessel to contend with, an unpredictable current and the sharks that he'd spotted as the fish thrashed in the water.

'Cut your line,' he yelled to Ken as the four fishermen looked over at the water in horror.

Jake ran down the steps pulling his shirt over his head, and kicked his shoes off before he jumped over the stainless-steel rail between the deck and the duckboard.

All he could think about was losing Jenni. He'd watched in disbelief as Leonora had fallen between the two boats and he'd known what Jenni would do even before she'd kicked off her shoes. She'd had no hesitation diving in. It was no one's fault. Cade had followed procedure; it was the rogue wave that had caused the woman to slip.

Cade had the tender idling about ten metres away from *Moonshine* and as Jake went to dive in, he saw Cade reach over the side of the tender. Jake's breath caught and he watched as the deckie lifted the dark-haired woman into the inflatable boat. Seconds later, Jenni pulled herself over the side and put her arms around the woman who was sitting on the middle seat. Cade gunned the throttle and the tender surged towards the back of *Moonshine.*

'Thank God.' Professor Ramsey supported himself on the railing as the tender approached. Jake put his hand on the man's shoulder. 'We'll get them on board, and see if we need to get medical attention. There's a small medical clinic on the island.'

'As long as we don't have to go in that small boat again,' the older man said.

'No, they'll come out to us if we need them.'

Cade approached slowly and they all watched the swell as it rose and fell a metre at a time. It had come from nowhere. Half an hour earlier the sea had glassed off, and there had been no wind.

Just the unpredictability of the sea.

'Now!' Jake yelled and he jumped into the tender as Cade brought it in close. The other men, including Tony, had come down to the back of the boat, and they helped Jake lift Leonora across from the rocking boat. Her husband put his arms around her and buried his face in her sodden hair.

'God, sweetheart. That was too close for comfort.'

'I'm alright, 'she said, although her teeth were chattering. 'Wet and cold, but I'm not hurt.' She turned to Cade and Jenni who were still in the boat. 'Thank you.'

Tony stepped forward with a blanket and assisted the couple to the bench seat on the aft deck, and the other men moved away to give them space. Jake sat with his arm around Jenni and waited for the rolling swell to pass. She looked up and met his gaze and held it as they waited for the boat to stop rocking. Finally, the sea flattened and she jumped from the tender to the duckboard.

Jake followed her and held out his arms and she fell into them. They stood there for a moment, Jenni's wet cheek against his bare chest.

'Don't you ever frighten me like that again, Jenni McDougal.'

She shook her head against his chest as she took in slow deep breaths.

'Are you okay?' he asked as he finally released her. 'I'm going to have to go and see to Leonora.'

'I'm fine. Just a bit shaken now that it's all over. Those sharks had me worried.'

'I want you to go up to my cabin and have a shower. Get warm. There's a spare robe in the cupboard behind the door.' Jake took her chin gently between his still-shaking fingers and looked down at her. Her eyes were dark and wide, and her wet eyelashes were clumped together but she was still beautiful. 'And then I want you to stay there and wait for me. Okay?'

She nodded, compliant for once. 'Okay,' she whispered. The look in her eyes gave him hope.

He kept hold of her with one arm as he turned. 'Tony, can you please help Jenni up to the master cabin while I look after Mrs Ramsey?'

'Sure, captain.'

'And then come back down and help Cade with the tender.'

'I'm fine,' Jenni protested. 'I can get there myself.'

Tony shook his head as Jake handed her over. 'Captain's orders, Jenni.'

***

As Jenni stood under the steaming hot water in Jake's bathroom reaction set in. Her legs were shaking, and she was shivering. It took a long time for the chills to pass; every time she closed her eyes she could feel the rough skin of the shark brush against her leg.

Maybe she wouldn't tell Jake that it had been so close to her. It had brushed against her leg just as she'd pushed herself into the inflatable boat.

Finally, she switched the taps off and stepped from the shower, wrapping herself in a thick fluffy towel. Now that she was warm and dry—and relatively calm again—she felt silly being up here and waiting for Jake as he'd instructed.

As she thought about going back to her own cabin, the door opened and Jake stepped inside. He shut it quietly behind him and leaned his back against it. His eyes were dark and hooded as he looked at her. Another shiver ran down her spine but this time it had nothing to do with fear or being cold.

'Jenni.' Jake's voice was low as he stepped over and took her arms. There was something in his voice that shook her as he linked his arms around her waist. Suddenly the robe seemed thin.

'I love you.'

She widened her eyes and her heart set up a thudding in her chest as she stared at him, her mouth dropping open.

'I've always loved you, Jen. From the time we were teenagers, and the whole time I was away from you.' Jake rested his forehead against hers. 'I never realised what it meant that I hadn't told you and that I was away from you all of that time. Not until you disappeared under the boat, and I thought I'd left it too late.'

Jenni pulled her head back and stared into his hazel eyes. She was so close she could see each gold fleck in his irises. His eyes were deep, and held something she hadn't seen for a long while. 'Jake, it's just a reaction. You're making more of the accident than you should. I was fine.' Suddenly she remembered Leonora. 'What about Leonora? Is she okay?'

'She's fine.'

'That's good.' She felt self-conscious having him so close. Shivers ran up and down her spine. She could smell his masculine smell and his hands were warm on her waist.

'They were both in the saloon having a brandy as I came up here.' He pulled her closer and his voice had steel in it. 'I know I'm probably scaring you because I don't know if you're ready for this. To hear what I want to say. What I have to say.'

'I think you've already said it.' Her voice shook as she looked up at him and something let go inside her heart as it beat painfully in her chest. She wasn't game to let that tendril of hope take root.

'Jenni?' The steel in his voice had been replaced by soft persuasion.

'Yes?'

'Can I kiss you?'

She answered with her lips instead of words, lifting her face to his.

Damn the consequences, damn the reason she was here. Jake was all that mattered. If she was honest with herself, he was all that had ever mattered.

Nothing else did. His actions as a teenager had set them apart, a fall off the path that she would have preferred he'd stayed on, but she could forgive him for that. He'd said that he loved her, and she knew she still loved him. She always had.

His lips were gentle at first, and Jenni sighed against Jake's mouth as he slid his hands beneath the robe and linked them around her back. Now his hands were burning hot against her skin as his tongue played along her bottom lip. As she opened her mouth to speak, he pressed his mouth harder on hers.

'No words,' he murmured against her lips. 'Not yet. Just feel with me.'

Jenni closed her eyes. It did feel so right. It was like coming home to the place she knew she'd always wanted to be. Her throat tightened and her eyes pricked with tears.

Happy tears.

She opened her eyes and pulled back. A smile was playing around Jake's lips and he pulled her even closer to him.

'Do you think you need to lie down?'

'I think I do.'

##

An hour later, Jake propped his head on his hand and looked down at Jenni. She was pressed against him from shoulder to toe, and her soft skin was warm against his. He'd left the boat on the anchor and once he'd ensured that Leonora was okay, he'd asked Cade to take the watch while he checked on Jenni. Tony was keeping an eye on Cade for him too because it had been a frightening experience for the deckie.

Jenni's cheeks were flushed with a rosy tinge and her eyes were heavy and slumberous as she looked back at him. Her warm breath puffed against his lips as he leaned down to kiss her. The last thing he wanted to do was leave her in his bed alone. But he was the captain and duty called.

She knew him too well.

'Duty calls?' she asked and as she stretched the sheet slipped off her chest, exposing a temptation.

He bit back a groan. They had waited a long time to sleep together, but it had been worth the wait. Lowering his head, he kissed her again, and reached down and grabbed her hand as her fingers trailed down his stomach, heading lower. . .

'Not again, you witch.'

Her giggle filled him with joy, an even deeper feeling than the physical expression of their love had given them.

'The witch from the fish shop. Are you sure you've made the right choice, Jake?'

'Oh, I'm sure. And I'm going to show you again later tonight.'

He sat up and swung his legs over the side of the bed. 'But you're right, duty calls. I have to go and relieve Cade. Tony said he can fill in for you tonight.'

Jenni sat up and pulled the sheet up. Her hair fell around her face, but she smiled as she looked up at him. 'Don't be silly. A bit of a dip in the Gulf? You run down and get my clothes for me, and I'll have a quick shower.'

'I'm going to have a quick one too.'

She raised her eyebrows and slid out of the other side of the bed. 'I'm going first.'

Needless to say, Jake was late relieving Cade from his watch.

Chapter Nineteen

The days passed quickly—way too quickly for Jenni. The days helping Jake make the charter successful were fun and she'd picked up the routine easily. Tony and Cade were good to work with, and she gradually learned how a tight crew worked together and helped each other out.

And looked out for each other.

The guests had settled into the routine, and many fish were caught. Once they'd left *Starshine* at the island, and headed over to the Limmen Bight, the sea was smoother and Leonora had been confident enough to go ashore in the tender again.

But it was the nights that were unforgettable. Jake had insisted that she move into the master cabin with him.

'It's not a problem,' he assured her. 'For all the guests know, we're a couple, and like you said, even Tony picked it up even before we knew it ourselves.' He had taken her to delightful places every night, and there hadn't been much sleep between watches.

'A skipper needs to get more sleep, wench,' he said one night as he fell into bed at midnight.

The hardest part had been the night watches, when Jake had left their bed every four hours to go on watch. But they hadn't done much talking, and Jenni was uncomfortable about that. There were things she wanted to say to Jake, to clear the air. If they were going to make a go of their relationship, there had to be honesty between them.

Complete honesty.

On the last night on board, Tony cooked a special dinner. A sumptuous feast of freshly caught coral trout, and potato bake. Jenni had helped in the galley during the afternoon while Jake was on watch as they headed back towards the coast after they'd caught up with *Starshine*. She'd learned how to make crème brulee, and had eaten too much licking out the bowl as she and Tony had laughed together in the kitchen.

'Next charter, I'll share my secret cheesecake recipe with you,' he said as she whipped the cream for the dessert.

Jenni shook her head. 'This was a one-off,' she said. 'I was just helping out. 'I start a job at the local school in a couple of weeks.' She stared out the open window to the sea; the thought of going back to being a teacher didn't appeal at all.

'That's a shame. You and Jake work really well together.' Tony opened the stove and glanced at her as he slid a loaf of bread in to warm. 'I thought you'd been doing this for a long time. You're a natural.'

'I love it. I think the sea is in my blood.'

'So why don't you think about staying?'

'You know,' she said thoughtfully. 'I might just think about that.' The thought of Jake going off on week-long—and sometimes longer charters—wasn't one that appealed. The thought of starting at a new school suddenly appealed even less. Maybe after the two terms, he'd take her on the boat as a hostess.

As long as they were still together.

Great sex was one thing, but they needed to talk. Jenni needed to tell Jake that she had forgotten and forgiven what he'd done. She loved him and didn't want to lose him again, but Jenni needed to know how he had been able to afford his boats.

Whatever Jake Jones had done, she would live with, but had to know the truth.

Dinner was fun, and the atmosphere was light. Jenni took a meal up to Cade in the wheelhouse and he nodded with a smile. 'Smells great, thanks.'

'Jake said to tell you he's going to relieve you early, so you can come down and have a couple of drinks.'

Cade put his thumb up. 'Beauty. He's a great skipper. One of the best charters I've ever worked on.'

'He is,' Jenni agreed as she left the wheelhouse. Jake *was* a good skipper. He was a people person; firm with the crew, and he was great with the guests. The six on board had already promised to book another trip.

'Return customers, that's what we want to see.' Jake put his arm around her as they walked up to the wheelhouse to take the eight p.m. watch.

'Careful,' she said balancing the two dishes of crème brulee in her hands.

They relieved Cade and Jake checked the instruments before he turned to his dessert. The vessel was travelling on autopilot until they came within sight of the coast.

All was quiet apart from the scraping of spoons on the plates for a few minutes.

'Tony was a great find,' Jake said as he put his empty plate on the bench top. He looked at her with a smile and held his arm out. Jenni put her empty dish next to his and squeezed onto the narrow seat beside him. 'It's been a great charter.' He dropped a kiss on the top of her head.

'In many ways,' she said. 'Except for Leonora going overboard. But even that had a happy ending. They said they're going to come again so no hard feelings there.' She looked up at Jake. 'Tony asked me if I was going to come again. It got me thinking.'

'Overrated, that is,' Jake said with a smile.

'What is?'

'Thinking,' he said. 'I'm much rather do this.'

Jenni shivered when Jake's lips found that sweet spot at the side of her neck. She sighed and leaned into his embrace. After a moment she spoke again. 'Seriously though, I do want to talk to you.'

'So what were you thinking about? I'll behave.' Jake stood and moved across to the other seat.

'Aw, you didn't have to do that.'

Jake sat back and folded his arms with a smile. Jenni looked at him, still unable to believe that they were a couple.

'So talk to me. I'm listening.'

'You might not like what I'm going to say.'

'Try me.' His smile made her insides curl, and Jenni reached out one hand and put it on Jake's firm thigh.

'That's not going to help me concentrate. Or are you trying to distract me?'

'What would you say if I thought being a hostess was a job I'd like to do again?'

'Really?' His grin was wide. 'I'd say you're hired. Next question?'

As she went to speak, a buzzer sounded and Jake leaned over and flicked a switch. 'Okay keep talking, but I have to drive the boat now. We've passed the way point where we come off autopilot. Rightio, you've got most of my attention.' He looked forward watching the water ahead.

Jenni put her head down. 'Jake? I think we need to be honest with each other. I was angry at you for a long time when you ran away, but I want you to know that I'm sorry for turning you away when you came to see me that last night.'

'I understood that. Eventually.'

Jenni looked up. Jake's jaw was set and a muscle twitched in his cheek as he stared ahead. He nodded without looking at her. 'Go on.'

'I want you to know that I can forget about what you did . . . and that . . .' She swallowed and bit her lip.

'And that?' he said.

'That I forgive you.'

Again, the muscle in his cheek twitched. 'That's very kind of you.' All humour had left Jake's voice and a strange feeling settled in Jenni's stomach.

'I know you must have had a very good reason.'

Jake sat still and looked down at the screen, not speaking as he entered coordinates onto the screen. Finally, he turned to her. 'I've very pleased that you think that. Is there anything else you want to say?'

'Yes.' Jenni swallowed again wondering how best to phrase her next question. 'You want to be with me, don't you, Jake? Like this isn't just a fling. We are . . . together?'

He reached out and took her hand and relief rushed through her. 'That's what you're worried about?'

'Some. But there's one more big thing I want to ask.' She relaxed as his fingers stroked her hand. 'I want to know . . . I need to know how you bought the boats. Where you got the money from?'

His hand let go of hers and he gripped the helm with both hands. When he turned to her, his eyes were shadowed. 'Why, Jenni? Do you think I stole . . . again?'

'I just want to know how you afforded all this.' She waved a hand around at the boat. 'They must be worth millions.'

'They are.' He nodded tersely. Flashing green and red lights flickered on the water ahead. 'I have to concentrate on steering us in now. Go to bed, Jenni. I'll talk to you later.'

Chapter Twenty

Five hours later Jake sat at the control panel in the wheelhouse staring ahead as *Moonshine* approached the mouth of the Norman River. Was it only a couple of weeks since he and Gus had arrived and travelled up the river to Second Chance Bay? He shook his head, it was ironic really, the name of the bay; he'd kidded himself he could have a second chance with Jenni, but he hadn't factored in her lack of trust.

Not that he could blame her really.

Cade had come up to relieve him on watch but he'd sent him away. 'We're not far off the coast. I'll do all night,' he'd told the young deckie.

Cade yawned and nodded before he headed back to his cabin. Jake sat there thinking. Over the years, he'd thought that Jenni would have quickly realised that he wouldn't have done what her father had accused him of. Hell, he'd even regretted listening to her father's threats and leaving town that day.

Now ten years later, she still thought he'd taken the money. And she was prepared to forgive him?

Well, she could take her bloody forgiveness, and leave him in peace.

He didn't need her. He wasn't good enough for her.

The problem was, what was he going to do? If she was going to stay in town, he didn't want to be there.

He might love her, but he couldn't be with someone who would doubt him so readily.

I just want to know how you afforded all this, she'd said.

Jake dropped his head onto the helm and tried to deal with the emptiness that sat hollow in his chest.

If there was no trust between them, there was no future.

***

Jenni lay in Jake's bed and waited for him to come down from the wheelhouse. She knew Cade was due to relieve him at midnight and she lay there awake and worrying when Jake didn't come. No, she was worried before then. The look on Jake's face had been bitter, and his voice had been cold.

She was sorry he'd reacted like that, but she wanted honesty between them. If he wasn't prepared to be honest and talk to her, there was no future for them.

He hadn't answered any of her questions, and she was pretty sure he wasn't going to. It was almost light when she drifted off to sleep, only to be woken by her phone buzzing as it came back into range. She glanced at the clock, it was just after five, and she was still alone in the bed.

There were a few text messages from Mum, telling her about the trip, and how much fun they were having. A couple of happy photos of Rick and Mum standing next to the van brought a smile to her face, but it disappeared quickly. After pulling on her shorts and shirt she had a quick wash, and pulled her hair back into a ponytail. Tony was already in the kitchen, and had started cleaning out the freezer.

'Do you ever sleep, Tony?' she asked forcing a smile to her face.

He shook his head and flicked a curious glance her way.

Jenni was absolutely miserable inside, but she was determined not to go up and see Jake. If he wanted her to know the truth, he could come and see her. He could make the first move.

He was the one in the wrong. He'd always been in the wrong.

Breakfast was served and cleaned up. Three hours later, farewells had been made Jenni's misery trebled as the guests disembarked. *Starshine* was a couple of hours behind them, so she decided to stay on board so she could say goodbye to Claudette. *Moonshine* was berthed at the public dock in town.

Working her way along each deck, she stripped the beds in the cabins and cleaned the bathrooms. Not sure what to do with the linen and towels—she had a feeling that it would go to the local laundrette—Jenni finally went in search of Jake.

She went slowly up the stairs to the wheelhouse, but it was empty. Cade had driven the bus to take the guests to the airport, and Tony was still in the galley. She went up to the master cabin and tapped on the door and when there was no answer she pushed it open quietly.

Maybe Jake had gone for a sleep?

But the cabin was empty. She walked back down to the galley, her sadness increasing with every step. 'Tony, have you seen Jake,' she asked quietly.

'I think he went for a walk. I saw him head towards town about an hour ago. Everything okay, sweets?'

Jenni shook her head and felt stupid when her eyes filled with tears. 'Do me a favour, Tony? Say goodbye to Claudette for me and say thanks for the help she gave me. I've got a few things I need to do in town and at home.' She blinked and smiled at the chef. 'Thanks for a great trip. I learned heaps. I'm sure I'll see you around town.'

'Or on your next hostess stint?' Tony put the dishcloth down and crossed the galley to the door. He opened his arms and hugged her. 'You take care of yourself, love.'

Jenni nodded and picked up the bag that she'd left near the back of the boat. With one last look at *Moonshine*, she put her head down and headed for the fish shop; she would borrow Matt's car and drive home across the bridge.

##

Jenni had managed to be bright and bubbly when she went to get Matt's car keys. Luckily the shop had been full and she'd said a quick hello, yes it was great, and I'll see you later, as she took his keys and hurried out. She was worried she was going to run into Jake, and the way she was feeling she didn't want to see him.

Not now, maybe not ever.

The house was empty without Mum, and there was no sign of Dane and Donny. She'd been so preoccupied in town, she hadn't even noticed if the two McDougal boats were in the river. She threw her bag into the laundry and kicked her shoes off. The house smelled musty and she walked into the kitchen expecting to see dirty dishes everywhere, but to her surprise the sink was clear.

Maybe the boys had been eating out. After filling the kettle and putting it on the gas for a coffee she didn't really want, Jenni wandered aimlessly around the house, opening windows to let the fresh air in.

Could she have handled the way she confronted Jake any better?

Or any worse?

She groaned and pushed open her bedroom door. She frowned as she noticed a buff-coloured envelope propped against her pillow. Picking it up, she turned it over. Her name was written on the front in Mum's loopy writing.

She walked back to the kitchen and put it on the table while she made her coffee. Pulling out a chair, she sat down and lifted the flap on the envelope.

The letter inside was from Mum, and Jenni's mouth opened as she quickly read what her mother had to say. She dropped the letter after she finished reading it before picking it back up and reading again slowly this time, trying to absorb the words on the paper.

Jen sweetheart,

This is hard to write but I have given the situation a lot of thought over the years, and again more so since you and Jake both came home to Second Chance Bay. I hope you will find it in your heart to forgive me. I know that you and Jake belong together, and when I've watched you both over the past days, I knew it was time to make sure you knew the truth.

The ideal situation would be if Jake told you, and you believed him. Trust is so important in a relationship. But I don't think Jake will ever tell you, because he wouldn't want to be the one to disillusion you.

I never had trust with your father. Oh, maybe in the early days, but it was his doing that led to this situation. Bob was a gambler. He lost most of our savings, and he lied about it. It's a wonder we didn't lose the house and the boats, but I think he was wise enough to stop when that threat got close each time.

Sweetheart, Jake didn't steal anything from us.

Ever.

It was a story made up by your father. Jake overheard him being threatened, and your father didn't know how much he'd heard. He was terrified that Jake would tell you, or worse, one of the boys. First off, he tried to pay Jake out and get him to leave town, but apparently Jake stood up to him.

So, I'm sorry to say, your father lied to the sergeant and had Jake run out of town. What was a young man to do? No one would believe his word against the word of a respected businessman.

I didn't find any of this out until your father was in hospital. And then it was too late. Jake had gone, and I didn't know where he was. You had gone, so I decided to let things lie so you didn't think badly of Dad.

I haven't told the boys yet, but I didn't want this to come between you and Jake.

Do what you have to do.

I love you,

Mum

Grief for the years that had been lost due to her father's lies filled Jenni until she thought she would burst. She picked up her coffee and focused on taking slow sips as she calmed herself.

Grief for the lonely death of Jake's mum, with her only son thousands of miles away across the sea.

Grief for the ten years she could have been with Jake.

Grief that her father would lie to her.

And worst of all, anger with herself that she could have ever believed Jake guilty of a crime he would never have committed.

And then she'd made it so much worse by saying trust was necessary to their future. She had demanded trust from Jake, without offering it in return.

No wonder he didn't want to be with her. No wonder he didn't want to speak to her.

Jenni put her head down on the table and cried for what she'd lost.

Chapter Twenty-One

The second weekend after the *Moonshine* charter had returned Jenni sat at the desk in her bedroom. It was the same desk where she'd done her homework in the days she'd been a student at the school where she was starting work tomorrow. She traced her fingers around the faded blue ink of the heart she'd drawn on her desk the week before Jake had fled. Two Js entwined in a circle inside the heart. The ink heart had always been hidden under a pile of books in those days; she'd been too shy and sensitive to risk Mum or her brothers seeing it.

Jenni stood with a sigh and left the desk clear as she placed the folder and textbook into her briefcase. Her future was uncertain; once the two terms were up—and she knew they were going to drag—she'd look for a job somewhere else.

It was the least she could do. Jake deserved to succeed in town, and if she hung around, he would always be reminded of the past and how no one— scrub that—how she hadn't trusted him. She closed her eyes thinking of the hurt in his eyes when she'd asked him about how he'd afforded the charter boats.

No trust. There was no true love without implicit trust.

For the first few days she'd hoped that maybe Jake would seek her out, but she knew him well. He was hurt and she had let him down. He would leave again; she had to tell him she was the one leaving this time. It was the only thing she could do to make up for her lack of trust.

Moonshine had disappeared, and she was scared Jake had left already because of her. One night a week after she'd come home Matt had stared at her as though she was crazy, when she finally summoned up the courage to mention Jake. The boys were watching the news; she'd offered to cook and Matt had wandered into the kitchen.

'You okay, sis?'

'Yep.'

'Ah, finally she speaks,' Matt said. 'We thought you had the shits with us, but we did tidy up before you came home.'

'You did.' Jenni ran the hot potatoes under the cold water for the salad she was making. 'Matt? Do you know where Jake and *Moonshine* have gone?'

He looked at her curiously. 'Yeah, they went straight out on another charter, the day after you came in. Didn't Jake tell you he was going?'

She shook her head. 'No. We didn't part on the best of terms.'

Matt shook his head. 'Jeez, you give that poor guy a hard time. How the heck did you both survive five days in each other's company?'

Heat raced up Jenni's neck and her cheeks burned. 'Very well, actually. Until I stuffed it up on the last night. I told him I forgave him for taking our money and then I asked him where he got his money from.'

'Jeez, Jenni. You sure know how to kick a guy.' Matt came over and put his hands on her shoulders. 'And did he tell you about his father? More to the point did he tell you about our wonderful father and what he did?'

'No. But I know about that now. About Dad lying. But how did you know about Jake's father?'

'Jake told me about his inheritance before you went out on the charter. But I also know he worked hard to get where he is today.'

Jenni frowned. 'But if he's on a charter, who's his hostess? Claudette was leaving as soon as we came in.'

Matt shrugged. 'As far as I know, Gus and Ryan went on the charter too. *Starshine's* around at the public dock, so I guess they did. A hostess doesn't have to be a woman, you know.'

'I know that. I wasn't thinking. I could have gone out again,' she said softly. 'I could have told him I was sorry. But I don't think he'll ever forgive me.'

Tears welled in her eyes, and Matt held his arms open for a hug. 'He'll come around, pipsqueak. 'He loves you. You'd have to be blind Freddie not to see that. The boys and I have bets going on how long it will take you two to realise that.'

'Really?'

Matt grinned. 'Don't worry, the odd bet with a brother is not gambling.'

'I know that.' Jenni lifted her chin as resolve filled her. 'No matter what happens, I have to tell Jake I'm sorry.'

***

'So what's crawled up your butt this trip?' Gus stared at Jake after he'd spoken sharply to Ryan when he spilled a bucket of water on the aft deck. 'You've been very short with the crew a couple of times. Not a good look, mate.'

'Nothing for you to worry about.' Jake turned from Gus but the older man's hand landed on his shoulder before he could walk away.

'When something impacts on the crew, and has you looking sour for ten days, I think it is.' Gus dropped his hand and his expression was sympathetic. 'I'm about to relieve Cade in the wheelhouse. You grab us both a coffee and come up. Ryan's got the fishing under control.'

Jake looked across at the aft deck; the fishermen had lines out and they were chatting. Ryan was on hand for any problems that might come up; it was a small charter with some serious fishermen who knew what they were doing and needed little assistance. They'd caught so many fish the men had already booked another trip for next Christmas.

He turned back to Gus. 'All right. Give me ten minutes.'

'And bring a couple of pieces of that cake that Tony was baking. Smelled pretty damn good. With cream and ice cream, please.'

'At this rate, we'll all put weight on.' Jake laughed as Gus walked up the stairs.

'But Tony's a bloody good chef. You hang on to him,' the older man called back.

Jake followed Gus's instructions and ten minutes later he pushed open the door of the wheelhouse with his shoulder, balancing the tray holding the cake and coffees.

He placed it carefully on the top of the console. 'I apologised to Ryan on the way up.'

Gus looked up from the chart he had spread out on the bench along the side of the small room. 'Good.'

Jake sat on the swivel chair in front of the helm and stared at the water. There was no wind and the expanse of flat silvery-blue sea stretched unbroken to the horizon. A huge flock of migratory birds created a shadow on the deck as they flew over *Moonshine*.

'Variegated whimbrels,' Jake said.

'Smart, aren't you?' Gus said with a grin and Jake couldn't help smiling back.

'Leonora Ramsay told me what some of the migrating birds were called.'

'It's good to see you smile. Now tell me what's wrong. Woman trouble, I'm guessing?'

Jake nodded.

'I thought so. One minute you and Jenni were all lovey-dovey, and then you haven't spoken her name once since we've been on board. She went very well as a hostess, I hear.'

'She did.'

'And?' Gus stared at him and Jake shrugged.

'It's a long story, mate, and it goes back ten years. In a nutshell, Jenni's father accused me of stealing money from their shop and ran me out of town. Jenni believed him and that's the end of the story.'

'Doesn't sound like it to me.'

'Okay. So then she wanted to know how I afforded the new boats.'

'And did you tell her?'

Jake lifted his head and stared at Gus. 'No.'

'So you let her assume that there was something underhand there?' Gus ran his hand over his grizzled face. 'Jesus, Jake. Of course she did. How long ago was it? Ten years? She would have been just a kid.'

'She was nineteen and we were seeing each other.'

'So of course she would have believed her old man. Did you deny it then?'

Jake shook his head. 'I tried to see her the night I left but she shut her bedroom window in my face.'

'So let me get this right. You were accused. You left town under a cloud. You come back a millionaire?'

'I guess so.' Jake picked up the coffee mug.

'And then when she asks you where you got your money, you didn't tell her about your own father? You let her think there was something shonky about your actions.'

'She should have trusted me.'

'Maybe she should have, but you didn't help the situation when you could have, did you?'

'I guess not.'

'It comes down to two things, Jake. Actually three.' Gus sat on the chair beside him and reached for his coffee. 'The first two are communication and honesty.'

'What's the third?' Jake was beginning to feel a bit better, listening to Gus's take on the situation.

'The most important one of all. Do you love Jenni?'

Chapter Twenty-Two

Jake brought *Moonshine* into the dock at the old house. The river was a deep green and the current swirled along the mangroves as the tide pushed in. The sky was clear, and the afternoon was warm, and he let that lighten his mood.

He loved Jenni McDougal and he wasn't going to let her go. They'd work it out. He would tell her the truth about his inheritance from his father. The inheritance had set him up and provided the deposit for him to go into business with his two silent partners and purchase his boats. He could deal with her thinking that he'd made a mistake as a young boy, so she didn't think badly of her father.

He changed from his uniform and slipped on his denim shorts and a clean T-shirt before he picked up the papers that he'd printed out in his cabin and put them in an envelope.

With a steady step and hope in his heart, Jake jumped off the boat onto the path, and headed for the McDougal house. The windows were wide open, but all was quiet. He walked around the back and tapped on the kitchen door.

There was no answer, so he pushed the door open and looked in.

She was sitting at the table, a mess of papers and books on the table top. As he pushed open the screen door Jenni looked up, her eyes red-rimmed and her cheeks wet with tears. Jake's heart almost stopped. He hurried over and crouched down beside her.

'What's wrong, Jen? Is everyone okay?'

She shook her head from side to side and didn't speak.

'Tell me, sweetheart. What's the matter?'

Her eyes welled with fresh tears and she looked down as one plopped onto his hand. Jake reached up and wiped the tears away with his thumb.

'Jake.' Her voice was husky. 'I'm sorry. I honestly didn't know, but I should have believed you. I should have trusted you. That's what it's all about, isn't it? I failed you. I let you down. And because of that and my father, you weren't here to look after your mum when she needed you most. I know what my father did. He lied to cover up his own failings.'

Jake pulled her to her feet and held her close rocking her, murmuring soothing sounds until she stopped crying.

'It's okay, baby. I'm sorry I left without seeing you, but all the anger of those days came back. I didn't think I was good enough for you.' Never would he tell her that her father had called him river trash and that had stayed with him for years. The irony was that his own father had come from a huge cattle property in Central Queensland.

Nowhere near a river.

'Oh, Jake. We've lost so much time. How can you ever forgive me? And my family?'

'There's nothing to forgive, babe. But there's two things you have to know. It's not about trust, it's about honesty. Three things actually.'

She lifted tear-filled eyes and pressed her lips to his mouth. 'You don't have to explain anything.'

'Yes.' He nodded. 'I want to tell you. My father didn't know about me until after Mum died. He'd been up here on a holiday, and I was the result of a summer fling. Mum knew he loved the land, and she didn't want to leave the sea, so she didn't ever tell him about me. She chose to be a single mother. That's something I have to deal with. But she contacted him when she was dying and then when he died, it turned out he left me a sizable chunk of money, and I bought the boats with it. I have a couple of partners too. You'll meet them soon.'

'Are they coming on a charter?'

Jake laughed and shook his head. 'No sweetheart, you're going to meet them on our honeymoon.'

'Honeymoon?' Her lips tilted in a watery smile, but his Jen was back.

'Shouldn't there be a proposal before a honeymoon?' she said.

Jake sat her back down on the chair and dropped to one knee. He held her eyes with his and put his right hand on his heart.

'Jenni McDougal, I've loved you since the first minute I saw you. You are in my heart, and you will be there while ever I have breath in my body. Will you marry me?'

Jake's eyes moistened as she reached down and put her hand over his heart. 'Jake Jones, I love you more than life itself. I always have and yes, I promise to love you forever.' Her face broke into a beautiful smile as she leaned down and rested her forehead against his. 'I don't think we need anything more formal than that, so tell me about this honeymoon.'

'Oh yes we do, your brothers would be after me, if there was no wedding.'

'Okay, that's true.' Jenni watched curiously as Jake pulled out the envelope he'd put into his pocket.

He handed it to her. 'I thought you might like to see Paris in the spring.'

Jenni's eyes widened as she opened the envelope.

'Oh my God,' she squealed. She waved the airline tickets in the air, and her delighted cries coupled with the slamming of a door and heavy footsteps as her three brothers walked into the kitchen.

'Hi Jake, good to see you're back. And to see you smiling for a change, Jenni,' Matt said as he went to the fridge. 'What's for dinner?'

Jake laughed at the look on Dane's and Donny's faces as Jenni replied.

'Ah, I think we might have snails and frogs' legs.'

'And French champagne,' Jake added as he pulled Jenni into his arms. 'We have something to celebrate.

He couldn't see the look on his future brothers-in-laws' faces as Jenni's lips met his, and quite frankly, Jake Jones didn't care.

THE END

If you enjoyed meeting the Douglas family, Her Outback Protector, Don's story, is the second one in this series...

When Don Douglas skippers an adventure cruise to the remote waterways of the Kimberleys, a new hostess joins the family charter boat. But Clare Templeton is in jeopardy... and Don steps in to keep her safe. Will his attraction to this beautiful woman break down the barriers Clare puts up at every turn?

Her Outback Protector
A teaser for you...

As the small plane banked to the right Claire Templeton leaned forward and pressed her face to the window. For the first time in three days of travelling and gradually changing her appearance in cheap motel rooms, a glimmer of confidence began deep within her.

Brisbane to Mackay. Mackay to Cairns. Cairns to Mt Isa.

And now the final leg of her trip to Second Chance Bay at the base of the Gulf of Carpentaria was almost over.

Maybe she'd done it. Claire hoped she had; her future depended on it.

She jumped as the voice of the pilot crackled into her headphones. 'You're in luck today, folks.'

The plane was small, and he'd handed each of the three passengers a set of headphones as they'd boarded in Mt Isa. It suited her; it meant she didn't have to interact with the other passengers, although they both looked harmless enough. An elderly woman clutching half a dozen Myers shopping bags, and a young man who had gone to sleep as soon as the plane had taken off. He didn't stir as the pilot's voice droned on.

'We're over Burketown now, and you can just see the tail end of the Morning Glory. She's late today. Usually passes over Karumba before dawn but if you look to the east'—he turned back to see if they were doing as he instructed— 'you can see those lovely big rolls of cloud.'

Claire peered at the cloud formation. It looked like long rolls of cotton wool. Not very wide but stretching as far as she could see. Quite impressive.

'The Morning Glory is unique to the Gulf of Carpentaria. It's not very wide but can stretch — sometimes in an almost perfectly straight line — for a thousand kilometres from one side of the gulf to the other. Bloody awesome, it is. I never get tired of seeing it.' He turned again and caught Claire's eye with a grin because she was the only one paying attention to him. 'They say the old codgers in the Burketown pub can smell it coming.'

Claire nodded and gave him a polite smile before she looked back to the window.

The plane began to descend, and she turned her attention to the narrow river snaking through the wetlands beneath them. A silver ribbon caught the early morning sun, and to her deep satisfaction, there was not one sign of habitation below.

Claire had researched her destination, very, very carefully. Second Chance Bay was a place that few people visited; it had little to attract it unless you were a fisherman, and she was highly unlikely to run into anyone who had heard of her.

Or so she hoped.

The last three days of keeping her head down and waiting for someone to recognise her had been exhausting. With a contented sigh, she sat back, and ignored the churning nerves in her stomach.

Her new life was ahead.

You can find HER OUTBACK PROTECTOR in print on Annie's tore or on Amazon.

https://annieseatonstore.ecwid.com/

Have you read . . . Annie's bestselling Whitsunday Dawn?

Whitsunday Dawn
July 2018

When Olivia Sheridan arrives in the Whitsundays as spokesperson for big mining company Sheridan Corp, it should be a straightforward presentation to the town about their proposed project. But when a handsome local fisherman shows her what ecological impact the proposal will have, Olivia is forced to question her father's motives in the project.

Struggling with newly divided loyalties, Olivia is thrown further into turmoil when she is mistaken for a woman who disappeared more than 60 years before. When it becomes clear that Captain Jay is also keeping secrets, Olivia realizes that there is more to these sunshine-soaked islands than she ever expected.

Seeking to uncover the truth, Olivia is drawn into a dangerous game where powerful businessmen will stop at nothing to ensure their plan goes ahead, even if that means eliminating her...

Against the epic Far North Queensland landscape, this is the story of two women, separated by history, drawn to Whitsunday Island where their futures will be changed forever.

Acknowledgments

A special thank you to my wonderful editor and critique partner, Susanne Bellamy.

You polish my sentences until they shine.

OTHER BOOKS from ANNIE

Whitsunday Dawn
Undara
Osprey Reef
East of Alice
Porter Sisters Series
Kakadu Sunset
Daintree
Diamond Sky
Hidden Valley
Larapinta
Kakadu Dawn
Pentecost Island Series
Pippa
Eliza
Nell
Tamsin
Evie
Cherry
Odessa
Sienna
Tess
Isla

The Augathella Girls Series
Outback Roads
Outback Sky
Outback Escape
Outback Wind
Outback Dawn
Outback Moonlight
Outback Dust
Outback Hope
An Augathella Surprise
An Augathella Baby
An Augathella Spring

Sunshine Coast Series
Waiting for Ana
The Trouble with Jack
Healing His Heart
Sunshine Coast Boxed Set

The Richards Brothers Series
The Trouble with Paradise
Marry in Haste
Outback Sunrise
Richards Brothers Boxed Set

Bondi Beach Love Series
Beach House
Beach Music
Beach Walk
Beach Dreams
The House on the Hill

Second Chance Bay Series
Her Outback Playboy
Her Outback Protector
Her Outback Haven
Her Outback Paradise
The McDougalls of Second Chance Bay Boxed Set

Love Across Time Series
Come Back to Me
Follow Me
Finding Home
The Threads that Bind
Love Across Time 1-4 Boxed Set

Bindarra Creek
Worth the Wait
Full Circle
Secrets of River Cottage
A Clever Christmas
A Place to Belong

Four Seasons Short and Sweet
Ten Days in Paradise
Follow the Sun

Others
Deadly Secrets
Adventures in Time
Silver Valley Witch
The Emerald Necklace
Christmas with the Boss
Her Christmas Star
An Aussie Christmas Duo (two Christmas novellas)

About the Author

2023: Winner of the long contemporary RUBY award for *Larapinta*

Finalist for the NZ KORU award 2018 and 2020.

Winner ...Best Established Author of the Year 2017 AUSROM

Long listed for the Sisters in Crime Davitt Awards 2016, 2017, 2018, 2019

Finalist in Book of the Year, Long Romance, RWA Ruby Awards 2016 *Kakadu Sunset*

Winner ...Best Established Author of the Year 2015 AUSROM

Winner ...Author of the Year 2014 AUSROM

Best Established Author, Ausrom Readers' Choice   2017

Book of the Year (Whitsunday Dawn) Ausrom Readers' Choice Awards 2018

Annie lives in Australia, on the beautiful north coast of New South Wales. She sits in her writing chair and looks out over the tranquil Pacific Ocean.

She has fulfilled her lifelong dream of becoming an author, and is producing books at a prolific rate.

She writes contemporary romance and loves telling the stories that always have a happily ever after. She lives with her very own hero of many years and they share their home with Toby, the naughtiest dog in the universe, and Barney, the rag doll kitten, who hides when the grandchildren come to visit.
Stay up to date with her latest releases at her website: http://www.annieseaton.net

If you would like to stay up to date with Annie's releases, subscribe to her newsletter on her website.